"But Dana and Aaron—a couple? I wasn't really thinking when I said that." Todd shook his head. "Let's be practical. Aaron and Dana have nothing in common. She's into rock music and art, and he's a total jock. She's hyper, and he's laid-back. They're like oil and water, Liz. They won't mix."

But Elizabeth knew that love didn't follow any rules. "Haven't you heard that opposites attract? Maybe if they had a little encouragement, Dana and Aaron could see beyond their differences and become friends."

Todd looked into Elizabeth's earnest, glowing eyes. "It would be an interesting experiment," he conceded.

"Let's do it," she urged.

"If Operation Pair-Up works, I'll grant you three wishes. If it doesn't you owe *me* three wishes."

"It's a deal," Elizabeth said. And she couldn't wait to collect her three wishes!

Bantam Books in the Sweet Valley High Series
Ask your bookseller for the books you have missed

SWEET VALLEY HIGH

THE LOVE BET

Written by
Kate William

Created by
FRANCINE PASCAL

BANTAM BOOKS
NEW YORK · TORONTO · LONDON · SYDNEY · AUCKLAND

RL6, IL age 12 and up

THE LOVE BET
A Bantam Book / September 1990

Sweet Valley High is a registered trademark of Francine Pascal

Conceived by Francine Pascal

Produced by Daniel Weiss Associates, Inc.
33 West 17th Street
New York, NY 10011

Cover art by James Mathewuse

ISBN 0-553-28618-8

Published simultaneously in the United States and Canada

Bantam Books are published by Bantam Books, a division of Bantam Doubleday Dell Publishing Group, Inc. Its trademark, consisting of the words "Bantam Books" and the portrayal of a rooster, is Registered in U.S. Patent and Trademark Office and in other countries. Marca Registrada. Bantam Books, 666 Fifth Avenue, New York, New York 10103

PRINTED IN THE UNITED STATES OF AMERICA

OPM   0 9 8 7 6 5 4 3 2 1

To Diane Schwemn

One

"Did you hear that, Liz?" Jessica Wakefield asked her twin. "There's going to be a new rock band at Sweet Valley High! Baja Beat. Isn't that a cool name? You *know* their songs are going to be great to dance to."

Jessica did a little shimmy. Elizabeth and the others within earshot at Patty Gilbert's party laughed. Everyone knew Jessica loved to dance. If there was music playing, she couldn't stand still.

Patty Gilbert, a tall, beautiful black girl and one of the most popular students at Sweet Valley High, was throwing an informal Friday night get-together to celebrate that her boyfriend, Jim Hollis, a freshman at Pacific College, was in town for the weekend.

1

Elizabeth turned to Patty. "Andy Jenkins is in Baja Beat, isn't he?" Andy dated Patty's cousin, Tracy, and they were both juniors at Sweet Valley High.

Patty nodded. "Andy formed the band," she told Elizabeth. "They've been playing together for a while, and they're finally ready to go public."

"It's going to be hard for them," remarked Penny Ayala. "The Droids have such a following in Sweet Valley. Their fans are very loyal."

"There's room for more than one band in town—right, Dana?" Patty smiled at Dana Larson, the lead singer of The Droids. "Besides, Baja Beat has a completely different sound."

"When will we get to hear them?" asked Patty's best friend, DeeDee Gordon.

"There may be a sneak preview tonight," Patty replied. "I know Andy brought along his guitar and a tape of the band's last practice session. Uh-oh—looks like we're running low on dip," she observed. "Be right back."

Patty and DeeDee headed for the kitchen to replenish the snack and soft drink supplies.

Jessica turned to Dana. "What *do* you think about Baja Beat? Aren't you worried about competition for The Droids?"

The tall, thin singer shrugged. "Not really.

There are a couple of other bands in town already. I think Patty's right—there's always room for more music in the world. Besides," Dana added, running a hand through her short blond hair, "if anything, I'll be glad for a diversion."

Elizabeth exchanged a look with Penny. She had a feeling she knew what was coming.

"Having more competition will give me an excuse to spend more time writing songs and performing with The Droids," Dana went on. "Since I gave up love, the band has really become my life!"

Elizabeth wasn't surprised by Dana's announcement. She had heard quite a bit lately about Dana's disillusionment with romance.

Jessica looked mystified, however. "Gave up love?" she repeated.

Jessica's question was just the encouragement Dana needed to launch into her favorite topic. "That's right," she declared. "I've had it with relationships! Since I stopped seeing Brent . . ." Dana paused.

Jessica gave Dana a cool look. She was the one who had fixed Dana up with Brent in the first place, and she hated it when her plans didn't work out.

"I've been looking for a new boyfriend, but

3

with no luck," Dana continued. "There's just no one out there for me!" She shrugged her shoulders.

"Sure there is. There's someone for everybody," Elizabeth countered.

"Well, I'm tired of looking for him," Dana replied. "It's not as if I haven't tried dating different guys. But between the musician types who are totally obsessed with themselves and the guys who have nothing to offer at all, I'm starting to wonder if it's worth the effort. If you ask me, love's completely overrated!"

Even though Jessica had fixed Dana up with Brent, she could understand her friend's position. Jessica herself had done a lot of dating, and she still hadn't found Mr. Right.

In Elizabeth's opinion, however, love was truly wonderful. She had had rocky times with her boyfriend, Todd Wilkins, in the past, but she had never given up on love. And these days she and Todd were happier than ever.

"I think you're wrong!" Elizabeth protested, and at the exact same time Jessica declared, "I know exactly what you mean!"

In spite of herself, Dana burst out laughing.

"What a surprise—the Wakefield twins actually *disagree* on something!" Penny observed.

Jessica and Elizabeth joined in the laughter.

4

Even though they were identical in appearance—both girls had silky blond hair and perfect size-six figures—the sixteen-year-old sisters had distinct and very different personalities and opinions. Elizabeth's playful sense of humor was balanced by a serious side. She was conscientious about all of her responsibilities, from schoolwork to her duties as a columnist for the Sweet Valley High newspaper. Her most cherished ambition was to be a successful writer.

Jessica approved of ambition as long as it was directed at something worth having—for instance, a funky new outfit or a date with a gorgeous guy. The academic aspect of school didn't interest her that much. She preferred social activities, such as cheerleading and her membership in the Pi Beta Alpha sorority.

For all their differences, however, the twins were extremely close. Jessica knew she could count on Elizabeth to bail her out of scrapes, and Elizabeth knew that Jessica would always be there when she needed her.

"I have an idea, Dana. Why don't you take out a personal ad?" Penny suggested playfully. "After all, it worked for Neil and me."

"You guys," Dana said. "I'm *serious*. I've given up on boys—and dating!"

"Well, I'm serious, too." Elizabeth still hoped

to persuade Dana to take a more optimistic outlook. "And I really believe that if you met the right person—"

"He doesn't exist!" Dana exclaimed. "I'm telling you, the last thing I want to do is get involved with anyone new. I've given up love, and that's final. I'll stick to my music. It's much more satisfying—and a lot less painful."

Todd Wilkins, Lynne Henry, and Lynne's boyfriend, Guy Chesney, approached the girls just in time to hear Dana's declaration of independence.

Lynne shook her head, and Guy laughed. As the keyboardist for The Droids and a good friend of Dana's, Guy had heard this speech before. "Complaining again, Dana?" he remarked.

Dana smiled. "I *am* starting to sound like a broken record," she acknowledged. "But love *is* pointless. I just think everyone should know!"

"So why don't you write a song about it?" Lynne suggested. Lynne herself had written a number of songs for the band.

Dana's brown eyes lit up. Hopping up from the couch, she tapped Andy Jenkins on the shoulder. A moment later, Dana was improvising a tune on Andy's acoustic guitar for an amused audience.

"I'm fed up with love," she sang in her

husky, distinctive voice. "Don't know what I was thinking of, letting romance fog my mind and waste my precious time. . . ."

Dana's silly, sarcastic song was a hit. In seconds, she had everyone at the party laughing. Or rather, everyone but Sweet Valley High soccer star Aaron Dallas.

Aaron stood alone at the snack table. He looked bored as he dragged a potato chip through a bowl of onion dip.

Their arms around each other, Elizabeth and Todd joined him. "Hey, buddy," Todd said cheerfully.

Aaron ignored the greeting. "You know, she's absolutely right," he declared.

"Who's right?" asked Elizabeth.

"Dana," Aaron replied. "Love stinks."

Elizabeth's glance met Todd's. *Oh, no, not another one!* her bemused expression said.

She knew Aaron hadn't been the same since his girlfriend, Heather Sanford, had moved away recently. He had dated a lot, in fact, he'd gone out with Jessica a few times, but he hadn't found anyone he wanted to get serious with.

"The world would be a much better place without it," Aaron went on. "I'm so sick of seeing happy couples everywhere I turn! And I hate the way all of my friends have to check

7

in with their girlfriends before they can do anything with me." Aaron eyed Todd severely. "It really bugs me!" Aaron folded his arms across his chest. "Nobody knows how to have fun anymore. Every single party in Sweet Valley turns into a makeout session."

Just then, Elizabeth noticed that the music had changed. As if to prove Aaron's point, Patty had put on a love song. Aaron, Elizabeth, and Todd watched as Jim took Patty in his arms. Everyone paired up for the slow dance—Penny and her steady boyfriend, Neil Freemount; Guy and Lynne; Andy and Tracy; DeeDee and her boyfriend Bill Chase, and even Jessica was dancing with one of Jim's friends. Everyone except Dana, who remained alone on the sofa in the corner, strumming softly on Andy's guitar.

"It's disgusting," Aaron said, sounding just as disillusioned as Dana had a few minutes earlier. "I think I'm going to start boycotting dating and parties, too!"

Before Todd or Elizabeth could say another word, Aaron had stormed off. It looked as if his boycott was starting right then and there!

The party broke up around midnight. Outside, Elizabeth and Todd climbed into his black BMW, and Todd started the engine. "I suppose

I have to take you home," he said with an exaggerated sigh.

Elizabeth checked her watch and then smiled. "Yes, you do," she agreed, "but not for another half an hour or so."

Todd grinned. "Just what I was hoping to hear!"

A few minutes later they were at Miller's Point. Above them, countless stars sparkled in the black velvet sky. Below were the twinkling lights of Sweet Valley.

The car windows were rolled down. A fragrant night breeze washed over Elizabeth and Todd as they shared a gentle kiss. With Todd's strong arms wrapped around her, Elizabeth felt both loved and lucky.

"We *are* a happy couple, aren't we?" she murmured.

Todd dropped a kiss on the top of her head. "You bet." He chuckled. "Poor Aaron. I told you he'd been complaining a lot lately."

"You weren't kidding." Elizabeth shook her head. "I don't know when I've heard him sound so—so cynical."

"Well, he's come full circle," said Todd. "He started out missing having a girlfriend, and now he claims a girlfriend is the last thing in the world he wants."

9

"Do you really think he's serious?" Elizabeth asked. "I'll bet if the right girl came along, he'd change his mind fast. I bet even Dana 'Fed Up with Love' Larson could fall in love again."

"Maybe we should get the two of them together!" Todd laughed. "We'd be doing everyone at Sweet Valley High a favor, sparing them all that moaning and groaning!"

The idea appealed immediately to Elizabeth. There was something irresistible about the thought of matching miserable Dana and miserable Aaron.

Who knows? she speculated. *If it works, maybe they won't be miserable anymore!* "I think you're onto something," she told Todd.

"Liz, I was only kidding—" Todd began.

Elizabeth cut him off. "No, it's perfect," she said. "Aaron and Dana both think they hate happy couples, but they'll feel differently once they're part of one again."

Todd laughed. Bending down, he brushed Elizabeth's lips with a soft kiss. "You're such a romantic," he said.

"What's wrong with that?" she asked. "I just want everybody to be as happy as I am."

"I know. But Dana and Aaron—a couple? I wasn't really thinking when I said that." Todd shook his head. "Let's be practical. Aaron and

Dana have nothing in common. She's into rock music and art, and he's a total jock. She's hyper, and he's laid-back. They're like oil and water, Liz. They won't mix. I mean, picture it!"

In her mind's eye, Elizabeth pictured Aaron and Dana together. Preppy, clean-cut, all-American Aaron and funky punk rocker Dana. Aaron in khakis and a crisp oxford-cloth shirt, Dana in a miniskirt, an oversize jacket, and glitter in her spiked hair. Todd was right—they did seem like opposites.

But Elizabeth knew that love didn't follow any rules. "Haven't you heard that opposites attract?" she reminded Todd. "Maybe if they had a little encouragement, Dana and Aaron could see beyond their differences and become friends."

Todd looked into Elizabeth's earnest, glowing eyes. "It would be an interesting experiment," he conceded.

"Let's do it," she urged, hugging him tightly as if to squeeze him into agreeing with her.

"OK, OK!" he gasped, laughing. "I'll go along with you. How are we going to manage it, though? Both Aaron and Dana have sworn off dating. How do you propose to get them together?"

Elizabeth frowned. Dana and Aaron did present a matchmaking challenge. "I guess we'll have to use a roundabout approach. Make that a devious one!"

"I guess I could be devious with you," Todd offered generously. "It seems harmless enough. But I still think Aaron and Dana are the least likely couple in town. And for that reason, Liz, I'd like to make a wager." His coffee-colored eyes twinkled. "If Operation Pair-Up works, as you say it will, I'll grant you three wishes. If it doesn't, you owe *me* three wishes."

"It's a deal," Elizabeth said, and she and Todd sealed the bet with a kiss. She was convinced that with a little outside help, the Aaron-Dana match would work. And she couldn't wait to collect on her three wishes!

Two

"Aaron and Dana?" said Olivia Davidson, unable to hide her surprise. "I mean, I like them both a lot, but—Aaron and *Dana*?"

Elizabeth, her best friend, Enid Rollins, and Penny had met at the school newspaper office during lunch period on the Monday after Patty Gilbert's party. As editor in chief of *The Oracle*, Penny spent just about every free moment at the office. Elizabeth, who wrote a weekly gossip column called "Eyes and Ears" as well as feature articles, could often be found there too. Today, however, they had a nonjournalistic project in the works. They were discussing Phase One of Operation Pair-Up.

Upon arriving at the office, the three girls had found Olivia, the arts editor of the paper, at work proofreading a movie review. Elizabeth had explained the plot to her in order to enlist her help.

Olivia's dubious reaction concerned Elizabeth. "Do you think they're too different to be a couple?" she asked Olivia, suddenly unsure she was doing the right thing.

"I can think of odder couples," Olivia conceded. "But at first I thought you'd picked their names out of a hat."

"Well, I did, sort of," Elizabeth admitted. "But they have one important thing in common—they're both fed up with love."

"The object is to change that by making them fall in love with each other," Penny explained, glancing at the clock. "Dana's going to be here any minute—we'd better get ready!"

Penny had a legitimate reason for asking Dana to stop by the newspaper office. She had written out the lyrics of Dana's song about giving up love and was going to print them in the next issue of *The Oracle* as a humor piece. Penny wanted Dana to look over the copy before it went to the typesetter.

"What exactly are we supposed to do?" Enid asked.

"Well, I think the best strategy is to start slowly," answered Elizabeth. "Todd and I figure it will only scare Dana and Aaron away from each other if we make any kind of obvious statement about fixing them up. So instead, we'll just drop a few suggestive remarks." Elizabeth perched on the edge of a desk as her friends gathered around her. "This is what's supposed to happen . . ."

A few minutes later the door of the office swung open. That was their cue.

The four girls were huddled close together, as planned. "Aaron was asking a million questions about Dana at Patty's party the other night," Elizabeth related in a conspiratorial tone. "I don't know what—" Elizabeth stopped talking abruptly as she pretended to notice Dana for the first time. She exchanged embarrassed looks with Enid, Penny, and Olivia, then casually said, "Oh, hi, Dana!"

Dana's eyes widened in surprise. She had heard what Elizabeth said about Aaron, Elizabeth guessed. But it was obvious that the remark was supposed to be a secret, so Dana was going to pretend she hadn't heard it.

Sure enough, Dana addressed them nonchalantly, as if she hadn't interrupted anything. "Hi, you guys. Do you want me to read the galleys on 'Fed Up with Love,' Penny?"

Penny went to her desk and flipped through

15

the galleys. "Here it is. Read it through and let me know if I got the words right. I'm taking the layouts to the printer this afternoon."

As Dana and Penny bent their heads to study the printed page, Elizabeth smiled triumphantly at Enid and Olivia.

Enid gave her a thumbs-up sign. "We've given her something to think about," she whispered.

"So far so good!" Elizabeth whispered back.

"So, are you guys ready?" Todd asked.

Neil Freemount and Winston Egbert nodded.

Gym class was about to start, and the three boys were changing into shorts and T-shirts in the locker room. Todd had just strolled casually past Aaron's locker two rows away to check out if Aaron was ready to head to the gym. Aaron had been lacing up his sneakers.

"If you ask me, this is nutty," Winston said.

"I agree," said Todd under his breath. "It'll never work. There's just no way Aaron and Dana will hit it off. But I promised Liz I'd help get the ball rolling."

"Penny's stuck on this idea, too," remarked Neil. "I guess since she met me she's turned into a hopeless romantic."

"Yeah, right!" Winston rolled his eyes.

Just then, they heard a locker door slam. It had to be Aaron's.

"Get set," Todd whispered. "We're on the air." Clearing his throat, he began speaking in a much louder voice. "Wait'll you hear this, guys." Todd stifled a laugh as Winston and Neil pretended to look interested. "I heard at lunch that Dana Larson has a major crush. You'll never guess who she has a crush on. . . ."

The timing was perfect. At that instant, Aaron reached the row of lockers where Todd, Winston, and Neil were talking.

"You're kidding!" Winston exclaimed, sounding as if he were reading from a script. "She likes *him*?"

As Aaron looked their way, Todd, Winston, and Neil shuffled their feet, coughed, and exchanged sly glances. "Uh, like I was saying, I hope we play volleyball today. I'm sick of hockey," said Todd.

"Me, too," agreed Winston quickly.

"Yeah, volleyball," Neil added.

Todd couldn't believe how stupid they all sounded. Aaron was never going to buy it!

Todd soon saw that he was wrong. As the four boys walked out of the locker room together, there was an unmistakable look of curiosity on Aaron's handsome face. At one point he opened his mouth as if he were about to ask the others something, but then he changed his mind.

He's curious about who Dana likes, and he thinks it might be him! Todd realized, marveling at how well the little charade had worked. He really hadn't expected Aaron to be interested. Todd looked at Neil and shrugged. Maybe Elizabeth and Penny were on the right track, after all!

On her way to the cafeteria for lunch the next day, Elizabeth cut through the main lobby of Sweet Valley High. She had just met with Todd, who had to swing by the library before lunch, and they had traded notes on Operation Pair-Up. Elizabeth smiled, recalling Todd's grudging admission that Aaron seemed to have responded to the idea that Dana might have a crush on him. Any boy would be flattered to think a gorgeous girl like Dana cared for him!

There's Dana now, Elizabeth observed as she neared the pay phones. Dana was waiting to make a call, leaning back against the wall with one foot tucked up. She was wearing a velvet miniskirt, with a cropped jacket, black tights, and lace-up ankle boots, and she looked fantastic.

Elizabeth slowed down, wondering if she should drop another hint about Aaron. As she considered it Aaron himself walked by.

Their reaction to each other as their eyes met was crystal clear. Dana's fair cheeks reddened, and Aaron, the boy who had said love stunk, actually blushed.

It was all the evidence Elizabeth needed. Phase One had been a complete success! Dana and Aaron were aware of each other in a new way. It was definitely time for Phase Two. But what was it going to involve?

Elizabeth hurried to the cafeteria, anxious to talk to her friends. The large, airy room was already packed with students talking and laughing, tossing lunch bags and aluminum foil balls around, and generally being rowdy.

After a few seconds, Elizabeth spotted Enid, Penny, and Olivia at a corner table. "Guess what I just saw!" she announced, coming up to their table. After relating the incident at the pay phone, she asked, "Do you all think it means what *I* think it means?"

Penny nodded, her eyes sparkling. "They both got the message, and they're intrigued."

19

Enid agreed. "People don't blush over people they don't find attractive. They yawn."

Elizabeth laughed. "You're right!"

"So, is that it?" Olivia asked. "You've got them thinking about each other. Are you going to leave the next move up to them?"

Elizabeth shook her head, her ponytail swinging back and forth. "No way. If we leave it up to them, there won't *be* a next move. They're involved in such different activities. I can't imagine that their paths cross very often. And they've both supposedly given up on relationships. They're not about to seek each other out and try to get to know each other better."

"So if they're not about to seek each other out . . ." Enid began.

"They have to be thrown together," Elizabeth concluded. "And since they've given up on the dating scene, it'll have to be a double date— one that doesn't *look* like a double date. Todd and I will have to trick them into coming along with us to a movie or something."

As she bit into her chicken salad sandwich, Elizabeth considered the situation. Maybe she and Todd could avoid lying outright. Elizabeth could invite Dana to the movies and mention that Todd might bring a friend.

Absorbed in her own thoughts, Elizabeth

didn't realize that Enid was watching her. "Why the wrinkled nose?" Enid asked.

Elizabeth patted her small, straight nose and laughed. "I don't know, Enid. I guess I feel a little funny playing the sneak."

"Maybe you should turn this project over to Jessica," Penny joked.

Elizabeth smiled ruefully. Jessica was well known for her devious tricks. "Jess doesn't know about any of this," she said. "The fewer people who do, the better. That way, there's less chance of Dana and Aaron finding out." Elizabeth's smile faded. "But what do you really think, Enid? Is all this deviousness OK?"

"Of course," Enid assured her. "Besides, it's not really deviousness. You're playing fairy godmother. It's for a good cause."

"It's perfectly harmless," Penny agreed. "What's the worst thing that could happen? Aaron and Dana don't hit it off."

"Aaron and Dana?"

Elizabeth, Penny, Enid, and Olivia looked up quickly. Jessica was standing there with a lunch tray in her hands and a surprised and curious expression on her face.

Jessica put down her tray and pulled an empty chair up to the table. "Since when is

21

anybody linking Aaron's name with Dana's?" she asked.

Elizabeth heaved a sigh. There was no way Jessica would let the subject drop, so she decided she might as well fill her in.

"Nobody—yet," Elizabeth answered. "But we're working on it."

"Why?" Jessica demanded. "I mean, I can't think of a more unlikely couple. Why don't you just fix up, say, Winston and Lila?"

The other girls giggled at the thought of a romance between Winston Egbert, the junior-class clown, and rich, snobby Lila Fowler.

"You are kidding, aren't you?" Jessica continued.

"Nope," said Elizabeth. "And I think you're wrong. Two people don't have to like all the same things in order to like each other. Dana and Aaron are both feeling cynical about relationships these days. I think they could change each other's minds about love."

Jessica's smirk changed to a scowl. "Since when does Aaron need you to fix him up with anybody, Liz? In case you haven't noticed, he has a perfectly fine social life. He goes out with a lot of girls, including me!"

Elizabeth could have predicted that response. She knew Jessica depended on Aaron to be part of the pool of attractive, unattached Sweet Valley boys she dived into for an occasional date. "Sorry, Jess, but that's just not true. Just because Aaron goes out a lot doesn't mean he isn't lonely. Casual dating isn't the same thing as meeting someone you can care deeply about."

Jessica folded her arms across her chest and narrowed her blue-green eyes. "So why Dana, of all people? Why not a girl you know Aaron could really fall for?"

"For example?" Elizabeth prompted.

"For example—me!"

Elizabeth laughed out loud. "That figures! You haven't exactly been dying to go out with Aaron lately, but you don't want anyone else to have him, either. Sorry. Operation Pair-Up has already gone into effect!"

"Well, it's going to bomb," Jessica predicted. She pushed her chair back, picked up her lunch tray, and walked away, trying to ignore her sister's laughter.

Not that I care about stupid old Aaron Dallas one way or the other, Jessica told herself as she wandered through the cafeteria, her eyes peeled for her friends. She didn't even care enough to try to mess up Elizabeth's silly Operation Pair-Up. Still, Dana Larson! Jessica felt a pang of jealousy as she imagined Aaron with the striking rock singer. Maybe it wasn't such a crazy match. After all, plenty of guys at Sweet Valley High thought Dana was a knockout.

Jessica spotted Lila and Amy Sutton at a table along the wall near the double doors. "What's new?" she called as she approached.

"This is what's new," said Amy, pointing to the wall. "Have you seen these posters?"

Jessica shook her head. As she set her tray down, she followed Amy's finger to a bright lime-green poster taped on the wall above their table. "A battle of the bands!" Jessica read out loud. "That sounds like fun." She pulled out a chair and sat down.

"More than fun," Lila pointed out, tossing her long, light brown hair to one side. "It's a challenge."

Jessica kept reading. Lila was right. According to the poster, three bands, including Andy Jenkins's new band, Baja Beat, had challenged The Droids to a contest in the high school gymnasium in a few weeks. Although not all the band members went to Sweet Valley High, they were all teenagers and lived in Sweet Valley. The contest was being sponsored by a local radio station. The best band would win an all-expense-paid weekend in L.A., where they would be the opening act at a hip music club!

"The Droids have been the most popular band around for ages," Amy remarked, taking a sip of her soda. "I wonder if any other band could really beat them."

Jessica nodded thoughtfully as she took a bite of her salad. The Droids *were* incredibly popular. But maybe it was time they moved over and gave the spotlight to someone else. Jessica's resentment of the Operation Pair-Up scheme eased somewhat when she pictured Dana's band losing to Baja Beat, Spontaneous Combustion, or the Suede Men. And why not get in on the action? she thought to herself.

"Let's get involved in the battle of the bands!" she proposed suddenly.

Lila raised an eyebrow. "What, form a band of our own and enter the contest?"

That was a pretty silly idea, Jessica thought. Besides, she had a better one. "We could be roadies," she declared. "You know, the people who help out the bands backstage."

"You've got to be kidding!" Lila exclaimed. "You mean lift things? Take orders?"

"What's the matter? Are you afraid you'll break a fingernail?" Jessica teased her.

"I'm not interested in slave labor," Lila said, "lugging around equipment and stuff. We wouldn't even get to appear onstage. It's a totally nonglamorous job!"

"You're exaggerating," said Jessica, taking another bite of salad. "I'm sure it's not very much work. And think about the fringe benefits! If we hook up with the right band and they win, we get to go to L.A. and mingle with real-live rock stars!"

The more Jessica thought about working for a rock band, the more fun it seemed. "Think of all the cute guys we'll meet," she said to Lila. "Rock musicians with long hair and tight black jeans—they're incredibly sexy. We might even meet Jamie Peters!"

Jessica could tell that Lila was wavering. Just a few days ago she and Lila had been drooling over pictures of rock legend Jamie Peters in the latest issue of *Rock and Roll* magazine while listening to his newest album on Lila's compact disc player. The two girls had agreed they would die for one glimpse of Jamie Peters in the flesh.

"Jamie Peters!" Amy exclaimed. "Forget it! He's totally over the hill. He's practically old enough to be your father!"

"He is not," Jessica denied hotly.

"He's a *man*," Lila breathed, her eyes dreamy.

"Well, count me out," said Amy. "I have better things to do with my time than hang around a bunch of rock 'n' roll deadbeats."

"You'll be sorry," Jessica said, wagging a finger at her. "Lila and I will win that trip to L.A. and meet everyone who's anyone in the music business!"

Amy laughed. "Fat chance!"

"Just wait and see—we'll be hanging out with Jamie Peters in no time," Jessica predicted. The tape she had heard of Baja Beat's music the other night at Patty's had been pretty hot. She figured they were the best bet to beat the boring old Droids.

She turned to Lila. "Let's not waste any time. Keep your eyes out for Andy Jenkins!"

Three

"A movie tonight? Let's see. . . . The Droids have practice after school so I'm free tonight. Sure, Liz, I'd love to," Dana said.

Elizabeth smiled warmly. "I thought you might go for it. The Plaza Theatre is showing *Adam's Rib*."

Dana loved old movies, and Katharine Hepburn and Spencer Tracy were two of her favorite film stars. She was a regular at the Plaza, a gorgeous art deco theater built in the 1920s that had been renovated and now showed classic old movies.

"Sounds great," Dana agreed. "Thanks for thinking of me."

"Oh, anytime," said Elizabeth.

Elizabeth had planned it so that she would

bump into Dana at the end of the school day on Wednesday. After Dana got her books from her locker, they walked outside together.

It was a gorgeous sunny day, and Elizabeth turned to Dana. "Do you want to sit for a few minutes and talk?" Elizabeth asked. "I don't feel like going straight home."

"Sure," Dana said. "I've got a little time before practice starts."

They chose a bench behind the school facing the sun. For a moment they sat silently with their eyes closed, basking in the warm rays.

"This feels great," Dana said at last. "I wish I could translate the sensation into music."

"I bet you could," said Elizabeth. "You really have a gift."

Dana shrugged, but Elizabeth's compliment pleased her. She did have something of a gift, Dana knew. According to her parents, she had been making music ever since she was a baby, when she rhythmically banged her spoon on her high chair.

"Have you written any new songs lately?" Elizabeth asked.

Dana tucked her legs underneath her. "A lot," she answered. "You've heard about the battle of the bands, right?"

Elizabeth nodded. "Everybody's talking about it."

"Well, we've decided to write all new songs to perform at it. Not that our old material isn't great. I love the songs the band has put together over the years."

"You just want to sound as new as the other bands," Elizabeth commented.

"Exactly. I'm really psyched for the contest. It's a chance for The Droids to stretch, move in new directions. And I'd love to win that gig in L.A.!"

Dana paused. She glanced at Elizabeth out of the corner of her eye. Should she tell Elizabeth the rest of the story?

It was true that she had been writing a lot of new songs lately. But Dana wasn't happy with any of them. They were all sad, bitter, or sarcastic—not the kind of songs that got people dancing in the aisles and won band contests.

And just that morning *The Oracle* had come out. Dana's "Fed Up with Love" had been printed on page three. All day long people had been coming up to her in the hall to tell her what a kick they'd gotten out of it.

Not exactly what I would have chosen as my signature song, Dana thought. "Fed Up with Love" was much too close to the truth. Reading it in

The Oracle, she had felt so exposed, as if everyone around her could look right into her heart and see the emptiness there.

A talented, independent woman doesn't need a man in order to feel complete! Dana silently chided herself. She had read that somewhere, and she tried to believe it—but lately she had felt as though something was missing in her life. Truthfully, she was tired of feeling so alone.

Elizabeth seemed to read Dana's mind. "So, Dana, are you still 'fed up with love'?" she asked.

"You bet," Dana declared, her tone firm. "It's the only way to be." If you were fed up with love, Dana thought, you didn't have any expectations, so you couldn't be disappointed.

At that instant, for some reason, an image of Aaron Dallas sprang into Dana's mind. Had she heard right the other day when she walked in on the conversation between Elizabeth and the other girls at the newspaper office? What did it matter, though, if Aaron Dallas had been asking about her? He was good-looking, but Dana was pretty sure that was about all there was to him. As a rule, she found sports types to be pretty uncultured. Still, as she speculated about Aaron, Dana felt her cheeks grow warm. He was cute—very cute.

Suddenly Dana stood up. "I think I'd better get to practice," she said. Gathering their books, she and Elizabeth turned their backs on the sunshine and headed toward the school parking lot.

"Todd and I will pick you up around seven, OK?" Elizabeth asked as she and Dana prepared to go their separate ways.

"I'll be ready," Dana replied.

"Todd might bring a friend along," Elizabeth added, as if it were an afterthought. "See you then!"

"OK—bye!" Dana called.

"Hop in!" Todd greeted Aaron.

Aaron climbed into the back of the BMW, then slammed the car door. Elizabeth turned in her seat to smile at Aaron as Todd backed out of the Dallases' driveway. "I'm glad you could come along, Aaron."

"Yeah, well, anything to get out of homework," Aaron said. "Although I should probably start studying for that big trig test one of these days."

Todd grunted. "Don't remind me! It's going to be a killer."

"A killer is right," Aaron told Elizabeth. "I've

never been good at math, but I have to keep my grades up because of soccer and— Whoa, Wilkins!" he called suddenly. "Wasn't that Enid's street? You missed the turn."

"Enid?" Todd asked.

"Yeah. I thought you said Enid was going with us."

Aaron saw Todd and Elizabeth exchange a glance. "I said Liz might ask a friend," Todd corrected him.

"I just assumed it was Enid," Aaron explained. "Olivia, then?"

"Actually, it's Dana Larson," said Elizabeth, with another look at Todd.

Dana Larson? Aaron stiffened. Dana Larson was going to the movies with them? He rolled down the window next to his seat. All of a sudden his face felt hot.

"That all right with you?" Todd asked.

"Sure. Why not?" Aaron struggled to sound nonchalant. Meanwhile, his palms started sweating.

Get a grip, Dallas, he instructed himself as Todd braked at a stoplight. *It's only Dana. She's just another girl.*

But Dana wasn't just another girl. She was a girl who had a crush on him. It had been obvious from the way Todd, Winston, and Neil

34

clammed up in the locker room earlier that week. And the way Dana blushed whenever Aaron passed her at school.

Aaron edged forward slightly on the seat, trying to get a glimpse of himself in the rearview mirror. His hair looked as if it hadn't been combed in a week. Aaron tried to pat it into place. When he caught Elizabeth peeking at him out of the corner of her eye, he pretended he was scratching his ear.

Sinking back in the seat, Aaron ran his hands over the knees of his jeans. He had on a faded old pair and a boring polo shirt. And Dana always looked great, even though he thought she dressed kind of strange most of the time. If he had known she was coming, he would have tried to wear something a little more interesting.

"Hey, Dallas, you still back there?" Todd practically shouted. "I said, do you want to study for the trig test together?"

"The test? Yeah, sure," Aaron mumbled. "Let's study together."

Todd made a remark to Elizabeth, and Aaron tuned back out of the conversation. He looked out the window instead, wishing Dana lived in the next town instead of just a few blocks away.

He had been to a party at her house, and he knew they were almost there.

Don't be stupid, Aaron told himself, taking a deep breath. *Lighten up!* Dana was the one who had a crush, not him. And it couldn't be a very serious crush, since she had proclaimed to the whole world that she was fed up with love. She wasn't looking for a boyfriend, never mind him. Todd had probably got the story wrong. The way rumors were passed around at Sweet Valley High, it wouldn't be the first time. And anyway, Aaron had made a resolution of his own. He was through with girls, except as friends, of course. He wasn't interested in being part of a couple.

Todd slowed down in front of the Larsons' house. Aaron quickly checked his hair in the mirror again. A few seconds later, the back door on the other side opened, and Dana stepped into the car. Aaron watched as Dana maneuvered her incredibly long—and incredibly gorgeous—legs into the backseat.

"Hi, Liz, and—" As Dana turned her head and met Aaron's eyes, the words seemed to die in her throat. She coughed. "Todd and Aaron. Great to see you."

"You, too," Aaron said, taking in her appearance with a fast, shy glance. She was wearing

36

tight, shiny knee-length black bicycle shorts and a big pink- and black-checked T-shirt. How did she carry it off? Aaron wondered. Any other girl would look foolish in an outfit like that. But Dana looked terrific—as good as a model.

Suddenly he realized he was staring. Now it was his turn to cough nervously. As Todd drove down the street, Aaron turned away and stared at the back of Elizabeth's head. Dana, meanwhile, seemed intrigued by the scenery passing by outside the window.

In the front seat, Elizabeth and Todd started to talk animatedly. The silence in the backseat was in stark contrast to the lively conversation up front. Aaron knew he should be making small talk, but he couldn't think of anything to say. It wasn't like him to be tongue-tied around girls, even girls as beautiful as Dana Larson. What had come over him?

"Pizza," Elizabeth whispered in Todd's ear as the movie ended and the theater lights went on. Pizza was as good an ice breaker as anything, and clearly there was still a lot of ice to be broken.

Aaron and Dana were very conscious of each

other, Elizabeth had observed with satisfaction. Conscious of each other—but not comfortable with each other. The silence between them on the way to the Plaza had been almost deafening. Elizabeth had started to wish she had never even thought of Operation Pair-Up.

Aaron and Dana had shared a tub of popcorn and a soft drink during the film, so Elizabeth figured that their hands must have brushed once or twice. That was a start, anyway. Now all she had to do was encourage them to follow up on it.

"You guys up for a Guido's large with everything on it?" Todd asked as the four of them ambled out of the theater.

Dana and Aaron glanced at each other, then looked away again. "Sure," Aaron agreed heartily, lifting up a hand to pat his hair for about the hundredth time that evening.

"I'm starved," Dana admitted, fiddling with the wide black ceramic bracelet on her left wrist.

Elizabeth knew she had made the right choice as soon as they were seated at a table by the waterfall at Guido's Pizza Palace. The warm Italian decor, the soft lights, the buzz of voices—it was all relaxing and casual. Everybody felt at home at Guido's.

"So, was the movie as wonderful as you remembered it, Dana?" Elizabeth asked as soon as they ordered.

Dana nodded. "It's like all the Hepburn-Tracy movies. The more times I see it, the more I like it. They had so much chemistry. No one else has ever come close."

"It's because they were in love in real life, right?" Aaron remarked. "So no matter what characters they were playing, their real-life relationship came through."

Dana's eyes lit up at Aaron's sensitive response. Elizabeth noticed and nudged Todd under the table with her foot.

"You're right," Dana said. She folded her arms on top of the table and leaned forward. "I suppose in the end there's a certain authentic warmth that no amount of good acting could replace."

"What I like about Hepburn and Tracy," Elizabeth interjected, "is how their on-screen romances are always a combination of love and tension. There's always some antagonism. In *Adam's Rib*, it's the battle of the sexes and the trial."

"So when they reunite it's that much more romantic," Dana agreed.

"It's because they respect each other," Aaron

commented. He filled his glass from the pitcher of cola that had just been delivered to their table, then raised the pitcher in Dana's direction. She nodded, and he filled her glass as well. "They clash all the time because they're equals."

"Exactly!" Dana smiled across the table at him. "I think *Adam's Rib* was ahead of its time when it was made. In it the woman is as strong as the man, and the man is as soft as the woman."

"But they're not totally similar," Aaron reminded her. He lifted his glass in a toast. "Like Spencer Tracy says at the end of the movie, '*Vive la différence!*' "

Dana laughed. Elizabeth kicked Todd under the table again. He met her eyes, and she could see he was as surprised as she was. This was turning out even better than Elizabeth had hoped!

Aaron's intelligent comments had clearly impressed Dana. He had shown her he was more than just a jock. Meanwhile, Dana was more relaxed and open than Elizabeth had seen her in ages. The two really seemed to be warming to each other.

Up until this moment, Elizabeth hadn't been entirely sure her plan was going to succeed, although she wouldn't have confessed her doubts to Todd. Now the differences that appeared to separate Dana and Aaron were dissolving right in front of Elizabeth's eyes. *They're a perfect couple!* she thought happily.

The pizza came, and there was a brief lull as they all dug in. It was obviously time for a new topic of conversation. Elizabeth was about to jump in and get things started again when Aaron did it for her.

"I've been wanting to tell you something, Dana," he began. "You know your new song, the one that was in the paper today? It's really on target," Aaron continued. "You're absolutely right—falling in love is the ultimate waste of time! Hepburn-Tracy movies aside, of course." He grinned at Dana.

Elizabeth nearly choked on her pizza. Of all the subjects Aaron could have raised! Now he was the one she wanted to kick!

Elizabeth held her breath and waited for Dana to react. For a few seconds, she didn't speak. A curious expression flickered across her face. What was she feeling? Elizabeth wondered. Could it be disappointment?

Whatever Dana's emotion, it passed in a flash. She smiled, but it was a controlled smile, and her laugh was brittle and dry. "No kidding!" Dana said, shaking her head. "That song came straight from my soul, believe me. If the best-looking, most talented guy in the world asked me out tomorrow, I'd turn him down flat. I have more important things to do!"

"Ditto," Aaron said. "With school and soccer and my friends, my life is pretty full."

"Mine, too," Dana agreed. "Of course, spending time with friends—like tonight—will always be a priority with me. But romance? Never again."

As Aaron and Dana turned their attention back to the pizza, Todd leaned forward and pretended to kiss Elizabeth. "Three wishes, huh?" Todd whispered in her ear. "Now that I think about it, my car needs to be washed and waxed. That's one . . ."

Elizabeth raised her glass to hide the frown on her face. There was no doubt about it— Operation Pair-Up had hit a major obstacle.

Four

"Didn't you say you were looking for Andy Jenkins, Jess? There he is," Elizabeth pointed out.

Jessica turned in her chair in time to see Andy step into the hot-lunch line. "Great!" she said.

"Why do you want to talk to him?" asked Elizabeth.

"Oh, it's nothing you'd be interested in, Liz," Jessica said in a haughty tone. "Now that you're so wrapped up in Dana Larson's life, I'm sure you don't have time for mine, too."

Jessica stood up, not giving her sister a chance to reply. She wanted to catch Andy before he disappeared into the crowd. She had been trying to talk to him since Monday.

Jessica approached the lunch line where Andy was waiting his turn and talking to his best friend, Neil Freemount. Suddenly a tall, stocky boy stepped in between Jessica and Andy. Jessica's nose wrinkled in distaste. Charlie Cashman—one of her least favorite people. Make that one of *everybody's* least favorite people. Jessica wondered if there was even one person at Sweet Valley High who liked that bully.

"Who are you trying to cut in front of?" Charlie demanded. The students sitting at nearby tables turned around at the sound of Charlie's loud, belligerent voice.

"I'm not cutting in front of anyone," said Andy calmly.

Charlie put one heavy hand on Andy's chest and pushed him. Andy staggered slightly but held his ground.

"You cut in front of *me*," Charlie insisted.

It was obvious to Jessica and everyone else who was watching that Andy had done no such thing. As usual, Charlie was starting a fight over nothing. "Hey, cool it, Charlie!" one of the other boys in line called.

"Give him a break, Cashman!" another advised.

Charlie didn't say anything else to Andy, but

he did force his way into the lunch line—right in front of Andy. Jessica had to admire Andy's composure. The handsome black boy simply took one step backward and resumed his conversation with Neil.

Jessica reached Andy's side. "What a jerk!" she declared, hoping Charlie could hear her. She'd like to see him try to push *her* around!

Andy smiled at Jessica and shrugged. "I don't care," he said. "The food tastes just as crummy no matter when it gets served to you."

Jessica laughed. "That's for sure! Andy, I have a question for you."

"What's that?" Andy asked, smiling.

"I was wondering if you were looking for any roadies for your new band. What with the battle of the bands coming up, you'll probably need some, and Lila and I really want to help you out," Jessica explained. "We know a lot about rock 'n' roll!"

"It would be fun to have you around, Jess," said Andy, "but I think my band has all the help it needs right now."

Jessica's face fell. "Oh. Well, thanks anyway."

"Wait a minute." Andy ran a hand thoughtfully through his short hair. "I think I heard something about Spy's roadies quitting. Would you be willing to work for another band?"

The light came back into Jessica's eyes. "Sure! Who's Spy?"

"Spy Lazarus. He has a band called Spontaneous Combustion," Neil said.

"Oh, I've heard of them." Jessica nodded. "They're playing in the battle of the bands, too."

"They sure are. And if the rumor's true, he'll be looking for help," said Andy. "I'd give him a call if I were you."

Jessica beamed her appreciation at Andy. Spontaneous Combustion—with a professional-sounding name like that, the band had to be good. She liked the name Spy, too. They were probably even better than Baja Beat. It sounded like the opportunity she and Lila were looking for!

"There's something about the Dairi Burger," observed Enid. "Even when I'm not that hungry, the minute I walk into this place I can't *live* without a double cheeseburger and fries!"

"I know," Dana said. "My downfall is their chocolate shake. I always tell myself I need one to soothe my throat after a rough singing workout." She laughed. "Yeah, right! Water would do that."

"I don't try to make excuses anymore," Elizabeth said. "I just give in."

Elizabeth had offered Dana and Enid a ride home after school. All three had voted for a pit stop at the Dairi Burger, Sweet Valley High's most popular hangout.

"Now I'm happy." Enid took a big bite out of her cheeseburger.

"Hey, Dana." Elizabeth was looking toward the take-out counter. "Isn't that the new girl in our history class?"

Both Enid and Dana turned to see. Dana nodded. "Claire somebody or other. Claire Middleton, I think."

"Hi, Claire," Elizabeth called without an instant's hesitation. The new girl turned, surprised. "Why don't you join us?" Elizabeth asked.

Dana smiled. Trust Elizabeth to act like a Welcome Wagon representative!

Her take-out bag in hand, Claire slowly walked toward their table. She kept her face somewhat averted, as if she wanted to hide behind her long, straight dark hair.

"We haven't really met, but I've seen you in history," Elizabeth greeted her with a friendly smile. "I'm Elizabeth Wakefield. This is Enid Rollins and Dana Larson. We're all juniors. You're new, aren't you?"

"Yes," said Claire, shifting her weight from one foot to the other.

Elizabeth scooted over in the booth to make room. "Would you like to sit down?"

Claire shook her head. "Thanks, but I have to go. It was nice meeting you," she mumbled. She hurried out of the restaurant.

Elizabeth stared after her. "I didn't mean to scare her off," she said in dismay.

"I don't think she needed any scaring," Dana remarked. "I think she's shy."

"Painfully shy," agreed Enid.

Elizabeth sighed. "It's hard enough being new in town. But if you're shy, it must be agony."

"We can try to include her another time," Enid suggested.

"Let's make a point of it," Elizabeth said. "She seems really nice."

Then Elizabeth looked at Dana. "I just remembered something, Dana. I probably shouldn't tell you this, but I think you might be interested. Last night, after we dropped you off on the way back from Guido's . . . well, the whole way over to his house, Aaron didn't stop talking—about *you*."

"Me?" Dana was taken aback. "You're kidding."

Elizabeth shook her head. "Nope. Todd and I both thought it was a little strange. I mean, Aaron has gone on and on so much lately about not wanting to date anymore. But from the sound of it, he really likes you."

Elizabeth and Enid munched on their french fries. Dana looked down at her own food. She knew they were waiting for her to respond. For the life of her, though, she didn't know how to.

She recalled the previous night: the movie, the pizza, and Aaron. When she first saw him in the car with Todd and Elizabeth, Dana had wanted to turn around and run. For some stupid reason, she had been incredibly conscious of him all through the movie—sitting so close to him had been very distracting. Then at Guido's she had expected him to be boring, and he had actually been interesting—smart and funny. When she was alone at home later, thoughts of the movie and her impressions of Aaron had mingled in Dana's brain along with the lyrics of "Fed Up with Love" until she fell asleep. It was very confusing. She didn't know what to think about Aaron's liking her.

Dana opened her mouth, about to confess to Elizabeth and Enid that she liked Aaron, too. Then she stopped herself. *I've sworn off love—I can't change my tune just like that. More than that, I don't want to change my tune!* Besides, Elizabeth had to have the story wrong. Aaron had said he was fed up with love, too, and Dana believed him.

"Aaron's not such a bad guy," she remarked, trying to sound nonchalant. "I think we could become friends. But that's it! There's no way I'd ever get involved with a dumb jock. I don't want to get involved with *anyone*, remember?"

Elizabeth and Enid both nodded. Apparently they accepted her answer. But Dana couldn't quite convince herself she wasn't interested in Aaron, no matter how hard she tried.

"Dallas, you are really out of it!" Todd observed that same afternoon. He and Aaron were studying for their trigonometry test at Todd's house. The kitchen table was scattered with papers on which they had been solving problems. Aaron had yet to solve one problem correctly.

"I know, I'm a space case today," he admitted. "I don't know what it is."

"Maybe you're just bored with cosines and tangents. I have something to tell you that you might be a lot more interested in. Last night, as soon as Liz got home, she got a phone call." Todd paused dramatically. "From Dana."

"Dana?" Aaron repeated, hoping he didn't sound as excited as he felt. What a coincidence—Dana was the reason he was having such a hard time concentrating on trigonometry.

"Yep. I guess she had a lot of fun at the movies—or, I mean, she had fun with *you*. It sounds as if Dana really likes you. She thinks you're not interested, though."

"Wow." Aaron could hardly believe what he was hearing. The rumor was true, then. He slumped down in his chair, his forehead creased with thought. Dana Larson liked him—that was pretty wild. It was great, in fact. Aaron closed his eyes and imagined Dana. She was so pretty, so funny and smart—and so determined to remain single and unattached!

"I don't get it," Aaron said. "If all that's true, then why doesn't she *act* like she likes me?"

For a moment, Todd appeared at a loss. "Um, well . . ." He hesitated. "It's probably because the two of you are so different. She's just not sure how things would work out between you. Plus, she's made this big deal about not wanting to get involved with someone, and she's probably embarrassed to say she's changed her mind. Besides," Todd pointed out, "you didn't exactly help much last night by bringing up that stupid song."

"True," Aaron admitted. He and Dana had really clicked—they'd had so much fun talking. The mood died as soon as he had mentioned "Fed Up with Love." Why had he, anyway? Why had he ruined a good time with a beautiful, intriguing girl? The first girl since Heather who had interested him?

He knew why. It was because Dana wasn't the only one who had a story to stick to. "Anyway, it doesn't matter," Aaron told Todd. "I'm not looking for a girlfriend."

Aaron sounded unconvincing even to himself, but Todd seemed to accept the statement. He didn't entirely drop the subject, though. "Nobody said you had to get married. Why don't you and Dana go out just as friends? That wouldn't be so horrible, would it?"

"Well . . ." *No, it wouldn't!* Aaron said to himself.

"I have an idea," Todd said. "Liz and I are

going to an outdoor jazz concert Saturday night in the park. Why don't you give Dana a call and go with us?"

"You think I should?" Aaron felt his resolve weakening.

"She loves music," Todd added.

"That's true. OK, I'll do it!" Aaron declared.

Todd's eyebrows shot up. He clearly wasn't expecting Aaron to change his mind so quickly.

"But don't forget, she and I are just going as friends. Just friends," Aaron insisted, to convince himself as much as Todd.

"Fine, whatever you say," Todd said with a shrug of his shoulders. "You're just friends. Now, let's get back to this trig, or you and I are going to *just* fail the test!"

After finishing her usual Saturday morning chores, Elizabeth phoned Dana. She told Dana she was just calling to chat, but actually she wanted to find out if Dana had gotten a call from Aaron, asking her to the jazz concert that night.

Dana didn't mention it, though. Elizabeth hoped that Aaron wasn't going to chicken out.

"Have a nice weekend," Elizabeth said after

a few minutes of conversation. "See you around."

"If you really want to see me around, I have an idea," Dana offered. "Why don't you come over to my house after lunch? The Droids needs to come up with new costumes for the battle of the bands. Since I'm the only one in the group who really cares about that sort of thing, they put me in charge. So I'm having a brainstorming session. Olivia and DeeDee have promised to lend me their artistic expertise. My cousin Sally's going to sit in on the session, too."

Elizabeth laughed. "I'm afraid I don't have any ideas to offer."

"That's OK," Dana said. "We'll be happy just to have your company!"

It struck Elizabeth as a good opportunity. If Aaron called while she was there, Elizabeth could observe Dana's reaction—*and* make sure Dana accepted the invitation. "I'll be there," she said. "Bye!"

A few hours later, Dana, Elizabeth, DeeDee, Sally, and Olivia were hanging out in the Larsons' cozy family room.

"This is what I'm thinking," Dana informed them. "The band's sound is evolving. Lately our music is becoming more funky and down to earth. That's why I'd like us to have a different look for the battle of the bands."

DeeDee tucked a pillow behind her back, then flipped open her sketchbook. "How about a jungle motif?" she suggested. "The band could wear shirts with tiger and leopard prints."

"And depending on whether or not you can use a backdrop, maybe you could use a curtain of long green vines," Olivia added. "That would work well, since your backdrop needs to be something you can set up easily and quickly."

"I like it!" Dana clapped her hands. "I'm glad I brought you guys in on this. It would have taken me all weekend to come up with something, and it wouldn't have been half as good!"

At that instant, the telephone on the end table rang, and Elizabeth jumped. She held her breath as Dana picked it up.

"This is Dana. Oh, hi, Aaron."

Elizabeth thought Dana's husky voice sounded a little bit on the high and nervous side. And there was no mistaking the blush on her face.

"Tonight? Actually, I *am* free. The band had a gig, but the place canceled on us. Jazz? Uh, sure. I'd love that." Dana glanced at Elizabeth, who tried to look as innocent as possible. "Eight o'clock's great. See you then."

Dana hung up the phone. "It looks like we're both going to the jazz concert, Liz," she remarked. She was acting casual, but the sparkle in her eyes told Elizabeth she was more than a little excited.

"Aaron asked you?" Elizabeth said, still playing dumb. "That'll be fun. We can sit together! Unless," she added, "you two want to be alone."

"No way!" Dana held up her hands. "I mean, this isn't a date or anything."

"It sounds like a date to me!" Olivia observed slyly.

"Well, it's not," Dana insisted. "We're just friends!"

Elizabeth turned to Olivia and winked. "Of course you are," she said. "Just friends."

Five

Jessica drummed her fingers on the butcher-block tabletop and studied the number she had circled in the phone book. There was only one Lazarus family listed in Sweet Valley—that had to be the one.

Do I really want to call him? she asked herself. After speaking with Andy, Jessica had been psyched to track down Spy Lazarus. The name wasn't familiar, but she just assumed that was because he ran with a different crowd. A *very* different—and very weird—crowd, she and Lila had learned when they asked around. Although he was a senior at Sweet Valley High, he hung out with guys who went to other schools or guys who had dropped out of high school.

Maybe it wasn't worth it, Jessica thought, closing the phone book but holding her place with one finger. After all, there was no guarantee that Spontaneous Combustion would win the contest and the weekend in L.A.!

Just then, Elizabeth breezed into the Spanish-tiled kitchen. "Hi, Jess! What are you up to?"

Jessica shrugged. "Nothing much. How about you? Have any big plans for the evening?"

Elizabeth opened the refrigerator and pulled out a pitcher of fresh-squeezed orange juice. "Actually, I do. There's an outdoor jazz concert in the park, and Todd and I are going."

"An outdoor jazz concert—that sounds like fun," Jessica commented, tapping the phone book. "I was looking for something to do tonight. How about if I come along?"

"Sorry, Jess," Elizabeth answered. "I wish you could, but it's a double date. We're going with Aaron and Dana. I think you'd feel kind of out of place."

Jessica couldn't believe her ears. How could her twin be so insensitive? By all rights, Dana should be the one feeling out of place, and Jessica should be Aaron's date! Instead, Jessica was supposed to miss out while Elizabeth bent over backward seeing to it that Dana Larson had a boyfriend.

Jessica glared at her sister. "Thanks anyway," she said sarcastically. "Go ahead—have a great time. I hope it rains!"

Elizabeth's eyes widened. "Jess, I didn't mean to hurt your feelings. Of course you can join us if you want."

"I don't want," Jessica snapped. "Believe me, I have better things to do," she said huffily as she reopened the phone book.

Yes, she had better things to do by far. She wasn't going to sit back and listen to boring jazz—she was going to be a part of the rock 'n' roll world.

Jessica reached for the telephone and quickly punched out the number. "Hello, may I speak to . . . Spy?"

"What a night for music under the stars!" Dana leaned back on her elbows and tipped her face toward the sky.

Elizabeth, Todd, Aaron, and Dana had spread a blanket on an open patch of grass not far from the gazebo where the jazz band would play. Overhead, the dark sky looked like soft black velvet, and the warm air was filled with the scent of flowers. A more romantic setting would have been hard to imagine.

But I'm not here for romance, Dana reminded herself. She sat up, wrapping her arms around her knees.

"I like to sing out of doors myself," she said in a more matter-of-fact tone. "It's the Woodstock thing, I guess. There's a hippie buried inside this punk rocker."

Dana waited for Aaron to make some kind of comment, but he didn't. She sighed. *He doesn't have any idea what I'm talking about. What does a jock know about music?*

She stole a glance at him. It almost looked as if he were there as Todd's date. He was sitting closer to Todd than Elizabeth was! Meanwhile, there was a good two feet of blanket between him and Dana.

He can't be that interested in me, Dana decided. Elizabeth had gotten the wrong idea somehow. Dana knew she should be relieved; she would have felt awkward if she thought Aaron liked her more than she liked him. But instead, she found herself wishing Aaron would at least try to put his arm around her. Of course, she wouldn't let him. She would give him a look that said, "We're just friends, remember?"

But if she and Aaron were just friends, then

why was her pulse racing? Only two things ever gave Dana this shaky feeling: performing—and being in love.

She snuck another look at Aaron. He was watching the gazebo, where the concert had begun. In the twilight, his chiseled profile was softer. The lock of dark hair falling forward on his forehead made him look young. Dana's fingers tingled. Suddenly she had a strong urge to reach out and touch him.

I'm attracted to him, she realized in amazement. *But why?* He wasn't even her type! Then Dana remembered. The reason she was fed up with love was because her type of guy had always turned out to be a disappointment. Maybe instead of simply giving up on love, she should try looking at love in a different way.

Dana shook these thoughts from her head. She had come to the park for music, not soul-searching.

The band was good. It was a group of local musicians who sounded very professional. Dana soon found herself tapping her feet. A few minutes later she noticed that Aaron was tapping his feet to the beat, too.

"Jazz is fun, isn't it?" she ventured. "It's a great change of pace from rock. It doesn't blast out your eardrums, either!"

"I don't know the first thing about jazz," Aaron admitted. He smiled ruefully. "There, the cat's out of the bag!"

"That's OK," Dana assured him. "I'm not exactly an expert myself. I know enough to know that there's a lot more I *don't* know. If that makes any sense!"

He laughed. "Yeah, it does. Well, you've still got a jump on me. So, clue me in. What is it I'm listening to here?"

"You want the history of jazz in forty words or less?" Dana laughed, but Aaron's interest pleased her.

"No, I want to know what *you* like about it," he said, his eyes intent on her.

Dana looked down at her tucked-up knees, glad it was dark so Aaron couldn't see her blush. "What do I like about jazz . . ." She thought for a moment and then said, "the emotion and the individuality, I guess. Innovation and rebellion are what jazz has been all about since the start. Even if the band plays some golden oldie, it can still sound new, mostly because of the solos. That's when one player steps out and improvises, finds a new way to interpret the music. So every player gets his or her turn to shine."

"It sounds kind of like soccer," Aaron

remarked. When Dana regarded him quizzically, he smiled wryly. "Does that seem like a stupid comparison to you?"

Now it was Dana's turn to make a confession. "Not necessarily. But I've never played soccer. I've never played any kind of team sport." She stopped short of telling him she never even went to watch the soccer and football games at school.

"Well, in a way, a soccer team is like a jazz band. There aren't supposed to be any stars."

"You're a star, though," said Dana. "I mean, that's what I hear."

Aaron shrugged. *The Oracle* likes to call me a star. I play a forward position, and so I get to score a lot—that's probably why. But there's a harmony to the way the team works together and everyone on the field plays a part. And when you get the ball, that's the solo." He grinned. "When you get the ball, you have a job to do, but you can also let your style show through."

"That's what soccer's really like?" asked Dana, surprised. "You mean it's not just a bunch of guys kicking around a ball?"

"Not in my opinion," said Aaron.

"Wow." Dana contemplated this new angle on soccer—and Aaron. "Sports and music! I would never have mentioned them in the same breath before."

"Me, either. All I know," said Aaron, "is that playing soccer makes me feel more alive than anything else does. I'm at my best when I play. I'm striving for perfection." He smiled crookedly, as if he were somewhat embarrassed by the sincerity of his confession. "Corny, huh?"

"Not at all," Dana assured him. "That's the way I feel when I sing and compose. Music allows me to exercise a special part of myself. It's what makes me *me*."

"And the battle of the bands . . ." Aaron winked at her. "It's kind of like the upcoming county soccer tournament, when you think about it."

Dana laughed. "I guess it is!"

All at once she realized that Aaron wasn't sitting a mile away anymore. At some point during their conversation, he had edged closer to her on the blanket. His shoulder was brushing hers.

Dana looked into Aaron's eyes. She knew she was staring. She was trying to discover more about his thoughts and feelings. Since Aaron was returning her steady gaze, she guessed he was trying to do the same.

"This is fun," Aaron said, turning away at

last. "I wasn't so sure about coming to this concert, but I'm glad I gave it—gave jazz, I mean— a chance."

"So am I," Dana said softly.

"I think they've forgotten all about us," Elizabeth observed in a low voice.

The concert was over, and she and Todd were walking hand in hand a few yards behind Dana and Aaron.

Todd had to agree. Aaron and Dana were walking very close to each other, talking animatedly. A connection of some sort had definitely been made. "It looks like you might win the bet after all," Todd said to Elizabeth. He shook his head. "I really didn't think Aaron was going to cooperate!"

Elizabeth smiled mischievously. "He's cooperating, all right. I think I'll start writing out my wish list!" she whispered.

Todd put an arm around Elizabeth's shoulders and gave her a squeeze. "Go easy on me."

"No way! You were the one who was going to make me wash and wax your car! I'm going to get my three wishes' worth of work out of you," she threatened.

They had reached the parking lot and Todd's

car. Aaron and Dana climbed into the backseat, still talking. What a contrast from just a few nights ago, Todd noted, when they had gone to the movies together. Aaron and Dana hadn't even looked at each other during that car ride, much less spoken!

"You mean, not only have you never played soccer, you've never even seen a game?" Aaron was saying in astonishment.

"Guilty as charged," said Dana.

"Well, we'll have to change that," declared Aaron. "Won't we, guys?"

"You talking to Liz and me?" Todd pretended to be stunned.

"Yeah, Wilkins, I'm talking to you," Aaron said, laughing. "Dana needs somebody to go with her to the next home match."

"Will you two let me tag along?" Dana asked.

The impossible had just happened—Dana Larson was taking an interest in sports. Todd glanced at Elizabeth. She was beaming. "Sure," she said.

"That way we'll be even," Aaron said to Dana. "You come to a game, and then I'll be at the battle of the bands when the time comes to cheer *you* on."

Todd checked his rearview mirror. It sounded as though Dana and Aaron were really falling for each other—and it looked that way, too. Then he saw the expression on Dana's face suddenly change.

"It's a deal," Dana told Aaron, but her tone wasn't as warm and enthusiastic as it had been a moment before. "After all," she continued, "*friends* should take an interest in each other."

Friends . . . The word hung heavily in the air. Dana had emphasized it. And if Todd had noticed her sudden change of attitude, he knew Aaron couldn't have missed it. Dana was obviously determined to stay unattached, even if she was having fun with Aaron.

Her remark effectively killed the lively conversation in the backseat. Aaron didn't make any reply.

Todd glanced at Elizabeth and shrugged. It looked like *he* was going to win the bet!

Six

"I never thought *I'd* be watching a sports event," Dana remarked to Elizabeth on Tuesday afternoon. The two girls had just taken seats in the bleachers overlooking the Sweet Valley High athletic field. "But look at me! I've practically joined the pep club."

Elizabeth laughed as Dana waved one of the little pom-poms the cheerleaders had been selling before the soccer game. "Should I tell Jessica her spot on the cheerleading squad is in danger?" she asked.

Dana grinned. "I do like to wear short skirts. But I'm not so sure about all that rah-rah stuff."

"Speaking of which . . ." Elizabeth pointed to the sidelines with her pom-pom. Jessica was starting up a rousing cheer. Dana didn't know the chant, but the rest of the students packed in the bleachers did, and they shouted along with Jessica at the top of their lungs.

Dana hadn't expected so much enthusiasm, but she found it contagious. As the Sweet Valley team members took their positions on the field, she leaned forward in her seat to get a better look. She spotted Aaron right away.

She had never seen him in his uniform. He was wearing shorts—and he looked fantastic.

"In case you haven't been following their season in *The Oracle*, the boys' soccer team is undefeated," Elizabeth informed Dana. "Aaron's the top scorer."

For some crazy reason, Dana felt a rush of pride at this fact. *Get real*, she chided herself. *You're not his girlfriend.*

"So what happens now?" Dana asked Elizabeth. "They're all just standing there like chessmen on a chessboard. What's the referee doing with the ball? Oh!"

The face-off happened so fast, Dana almost missed it. All at once the uniformed figures were in motion. As Aaron swept the ball away from the Big Mesa forward, his teammates spread out across the field, ready to support him.

"Aaron's good at that," Elizabeth said. "He almost never loses a face-off."

Dana held her breath. Aaron still had the ball at his feet. It looked as though he was going to make it all the way to the goal! Just ten seconds into the game and he was going to score! An instant later the ball was flying in the opposite direction. Aaron trotted after the Big Mesa player who now had the ball, but he didn't run past midfield. Dana knew, from what Elizabeth had told her, that it was the responsibility of the defensive players to get the ball back to him. She recalled her conversation with Aaron at the jazz concert and smiled. He'd just had a brief solo, and now it was somebody else's turn.

There was some fancy footwork. The Big Mesa player outdodged his Sweet Valley opponent and took a shot at a goal. Everyone in the bleachers leapt out of their seats, including Dana and Elizabeth. The kick was so powerful, so direct, it had to go in! Then Dana's groan changed into a gleeful shout. The Sweet Valley goalie had blocked the shot!

She sank back into her seat, thinking that perhaps now the two teams would take a break—and the fans would have a chance to catch their breath. Instead, the ball was tossed right back out onto the field. "This is amazing!" she exclaimed. "Don't they ever stop?"

"Hardly ever," said Elizabeth. "It's not like football. The same players stay in for almost the whole game. They have to have an incredible amount of stamina."

"I'll say," Dana breathed. No wonder Aaron had such great muscles. . . .

She located him on the field just as he received a pass from one of his teammates. This time his agility foiled the Big Mesa defense. In a few seconds he had the ball within scoring distance. His arms out for balance, Aaron brought his right leg swiftly back for the kick. The ball rocketed toward the upper left-hand corner of the net. It was in!

Dana jumped up. "He got a goal!" she yelled, waving her pom-pom. "We're winning!"

"It won't be the last time he scores, either!" Elizabeth predicted. "Wait and see."

Elizabeth was right. By halftime, Aaron had scored another goal, and so had one of his teammates. Sweet Valley was leading, 3–2. As the players gathered at their respective benches to get feedback from their coaches, Dana let out a huge sigh. For forty-five minutes, she had been keyed up tighter than a guitar string!

"I never thought I could get so excited about

a bunch of boys kicking a ball around a field!"
she confessed to Elizabeth as they bought soft
drinks at the pep club's concession stand.

"There's a lot more to it than you'd think,
isn't there?" Elizabeth agreed.

Dana nodded. She could imagine how Aaron
felt out there. Invigorated, full of strength and
energy and magic—the same way she felt when
she was onstage, performing with The Droids.
It was like a bond between them.

Back at her seat in the bleachers, Dana looked
down at the huddle of Sweet Valley players. To
her surprise, someone was looking back up at
her. Aaron smiled at her, and Dana lifted her
hand in a small wave, a flush of pleasure illumi-
nating her face.

Dana saw Elizabeth giving her a curious look,
but this time Dana didn't make any excuses.
She wasn't going to say that she and Aaron
were just friends taking a friendly interest in
each other. She wasn't going to crawl back into
her cynical, detached shell and start reciting
"Fed Up with Love" again. Dana didn't say
anything at all; she knew her happy expression
spoke for her.

Ever since that first night at the movies with
Aaron, Dana's feelings had been swinging up
and down, back and forth. *We're just friends,*

she had kept reminding herself. She didn't want anything more from Aaron, and he didn't want anything more from her. If he talked a lot about her with Todd and Elizabeth, well, he was probably just being friendly.

But the way Aaron turned to look up at her before heading back out onto the field for the second half of the game, and the way that look made her feel. . . . She couldn't deny that she wanted them to be *more* than friends.

Dana decided it was time to write a new song about love. In the last week and a half, her heart had opened up again. And the next time she had a chance to get close to Aaron, she told herself sternly, she wasn't going to back away as she had after the jazz concert! She just hoped he had changed his mind, too. . . .

Todd had arrived late at the soccer game. When he couldn't find Elizabeth and Dana, he had grabbed a seat with Winston, Neil, and some other friends.

Now that the game was over, people started to leave the bleachers, and Todd finally spotted Elizabeth. She pointed in the direction of the parking lot, and he nodded.

"What are you two signaling about?" asked Dana.

"It's kind of an informal tradition for everybody to meet at the Dairi Burger after a victory, including the team," Elizabeth explained. "I didn't want Todd to leave without us. That is, if you want to go. Maybe you've had enough of the sports scene for one day!"

Elizabeth watched Dana's face closely as she spoke. When the game ended, Dana had seemed almost let down, despite the fact that Sweet Valley High had won by a score of 6–2 and Aaron had scored three goals. Elizabeth wondered if Dana was actually sorry it was over.

As soon as Elizabeth mentioned the Dairi Burger and the fact that the soccer team would be there, Dana's eyes brightened. "Sure, I'd love to go! I want to give Aaron my congratulations," she added.

Elizabeth smiled. "I know he'd like that."

The Dairi Burger was already packed when Todd, Elizabeth, Dana, Neil, Winston, and his girlfriend Maria Santelli arrived.

They found space to stand alongside the take-out counter. "How convenient!" Winston observed. "Since we're here, we might as well eat! What's everybody having?"

They all ordered hamburgers, French fries, and milk shakes—everyone except Dana. She claimed she wasn't hungry, and by the way she kept her eyes fixed on the door to the restaurant, Elizabeth guessed food was the last thing on Dana's mind. She was too busy thinking about Aaron! Elizabeth couldn't believe it.

They didn't have to wait long. Their food had just been handed across the counter when the door swung open and a jubilant pack of freshly showered soccer players poured into the Dairi Burger.

There were whoops and hugs and high-fives. After asking Winston and Neil to claim a booth and guard the food, Elizabeth, Dana, Maria, and Todd pushed their way through the crowd to Aaron's side. Todd slapped him on the back. "Great game, Dallas!"

Aaron turned around, a broad grin on his face. "Thanks. It was one of those great days, you know? We had all the right moves."

Aaron was addressing Todd, but Elizabeth couldn't help noticing that he was staring at Dana.

Elizabeth withheld her own congratulations for a moment, giving Dana a chance to speak first.

"So, what's the verdict?" Aaron asked Dana.

He looked very handsome, Elizabeth thought, with his dark hair wet and slicked back. "Does soccer get the thumbs-up, or should I take up jazz?"

"The game was wonderful," Dana breathed. "I had so much fun! I never imagined—it was actually beautiful to watch. And that last goal of yours . . ."

"It was the best, wasn't it?" said Aaron. "You know. . ." He lowered his voice, but Elizabeth could still hear him. "It made a difference to me, knowing you were watching—whoa, guys! Take it easy!"

Dana, Maria, and Elizabeth were elbowed out of the way as another group of Aaron's buddies surrounded him in a congratulatory huddle.

"We might as well sit down," Elizabeth said to Dana, "and eat the fries before they get cold. Aaron's the hero of the day—he's going to be busy for a while."

Elizabeth, Todd, Maria, and Dana guarded the table, giving Winston and Neil a chance to join the celebration.

"He really played well, didn't he?" Dana said. "He's the best player on the team, by far. He's so fast, and he can kick farther than anybody!"

Elizabeth checked Todd for a reaction to

Dana's enthusiasm. He had missed her pom-pom waving and cheering at the game.

He appeared surprised, to say the least. "You really liked watching soccer? I figured you'd be bored."

"Bored?" exclaimed Dana. "Not at all! It was thrilling. When Aaron intercepted that pass by stopping the ball with his forehead—I've never seen anything like it! Talk about skill! And the last goal he scored—I bet most people would have missed that shot. The angle was unbelievable!"

Dana turned her head to look toward the soccer players and their fans. Elizabeth followed her friend's gaze in time to intercept a look between Dana and Aaron. It wasn't just a quick glance, either. It was a long, lingering look, and when Dana faced the table again, her face was glowing.

Elizabeth took a sip of her chocolate shake to hide her smile. The impossible had happened. Operation Pair-Up had worked, and Dana and Aaron were falling in love!

From the looks of things, Elizabeth and Todd's role in the romance was almost concluded. There was a new play at the Civic Center everyone was excited about. *We'll get four tickets and all go together*, Elizabeth decided. That would be the last push. Then the spark would finally turn into a flame.

After that, Elizabeth had a feeling Aaron and Dana would be making their own dates!

Seven

"He lives *where*?" Lila squawked.

"Wentworth Avenue," Jessica repeated as she braked the red Fiat at a stoplight a few blocks away from Fowler Crest, the mansion where Lila lived with her divorced father. It was Tuesday afternoon, and they were on their way to meet Spy for the first time.

"That's in the worst part of town! It could be dangerous," Lila declared.

"Look, Lila, I don't like the sound of it any more than you do," Jessica admitted. "But Spy's expecting us. We can't just blow him off!"

"I don't see why not," Lila said. "I mean, we don't even know the guy. It's not like his feelings would be hurt or anything."

"But I told you what he said when I called

him on Saturday. Spontaneous Combustion is absolutely desperate for help. Spy signed us sight unseen, even though we don't have any previous experience! We couldn't hope for more than that—it's the break we need," Jessica insisted.

Lila sighed loudly. "I suppose."

They left downtown Sweet Valley behind, and soon Jessica was turning the car onto Wentworth Avenue. Many of the small houses were ramshackle and in need of paint.

Jessica glanced at Lila. She was looking out the window, her perfect nose wrinkled in distaste. "I'm not so sure about this, Jess. Let's turn back!"

"Sorry. U-turns are illegal," Jessica said breezily. She wasn't going to admit that the neighborhood gave her the creeps, too. "Anyway, what difference does it make where Spy lives? His voice was incredibly sexy on the phone. Rock musicians are usually gorgeous. You know you go for their long hair."

"Yeah, I guess," Lila said. "But if he's so gorgeous, why haven't we ever noticed him at school?"

That's a good point, Jessica thought, but she wasn't going to admit Lila might be right. "Probably because he's too busy with his band," she said. "It'll be fun," Jessica went on, partly because she was nervous. "We'll be part of a real-live rock band! Spontaneous Combustion will definitely win the battle of the bands. They could even make it to the big time! And we'll be right there with them. We'll be in L.A. when Spy and the others meet all kinds of music celebrities. You know it's the only way, Lila. Your dad might be able to introduce you to a few movie stars, but he's never going to be moving in the same circles as Jamie Peters."

Lila couldn't argue with that. "This Spy person had just better be hot," she warned.

"If he looks anything like he sounds, he will be," Jessica predicted. "I tell you what. I'll be an incredibly generous, unselfish friend and give you first dibs on him!"

"Thanks," Lila said loftily, "but if he has eyes, I won't need your help."

Jessica laughed. "That's what I like about you, Lila. You're so *modest*. Hey, what did that mailbox say? Two fifty-six? This is it!"

She pulled into the driveway. The Lazarus house was no castle, but Jessica was relieved to see that it had a coat of fresh paint and the yard was well tended. "This is going to turn out great," she declared with renewed confidence. "Come on!"

The two girls climbed the steps to the front porch and rang the bell. Half a minute passed and no one appeared. "Nobody's home. What a shame," said Lila, tugging at Jessica's arm. "Let's go."

"Hold on!" Jessica pushed the button again. "Spy and the band probably practice in the basement. Give him a few seconds."

"One, two, three," Lila counted. "That's a few seconds. Now, let's—"

Just then, the door swung open. A tall, scrawny guy with very pale skin and dark, greasy hair stared out at them. A lit cigarette dangled from his lip.

Jessica saw Lila's mouth drop open. It appeared that Jessica was going to have to do the talking. "Uh—uh—is Spy home?" Jessica stammered.

"You're looking at him, man." To Jessica's utter dismay, it was the same voice from the phone call. Spy took a drag from his cigarette and blew the smoke back in their faces. Then he grinned. "Hey, you must be the Wakefield and Fowler chicks! Excellent! Come on in."

"Chicks?" Lila whispered fiercely as they stepped into the front hall.

Jessica shrugged helplessly.

"This way. You've gotta meet the rest of the

band," Spy was saying. "Man, are they going to be psyched to see you! We always wanted babes for roadies."

Lila squeezed Jessica's arm tightly. "*What* did he say?"

Jessica ignored her. *Think positive,* she told herself. Maybe Spy wasn't exactly what she expected, but that didn't necessarily mean the *rest* of the band was unattractive.

When she reached the bottom of the basement stairs, however, Jessica saw she was wrong. Calling these guys unattractive would actually be a compliment. Hideous was more like it.

"Dudes, meet chicks!" Spy said cheerfully. "Jessica and Lila, this is Hal, Wheels, Pete, and Motorhead. You can call him Motor."

"*Motor?*" Lila echoed.

"Yeah, when he's not messing with his guitar, he likes to mess with engines," Spy explained. "Got a car that needs fixing?"

Lila shook her head. Jessica fought back a giggle as she pictured Motor tinkering with one of Mr. Fowler's European sports cars. The situation really wasn't funny, however. Hal, Wheels, Pete, and Motorhead might as well have been Spy's brothers. For all Jessica knew, they *were* his brothers. They all looked as if they hadn't seen the sun since childhood, and they certainly didn't lift weights. Their arms were skinnier than hers! And their hair . . .

Lila was thinking the same thing. "Long hair, sure," she whispered in Jessica's ear. "And it hasn't been washed in a year!"

Jessica grimaced. It was starting to look as if she had made a big mistake. The band members surrounded Jessica and Lila, and Spy launched into an introductory speech about the various instruments and the special handling they required. All escape routes were blocked. Not that Jessica was tempted to make a run for it. Spy was a little spooky. She had no desire to make him mad.

Besides, she and Lila might be able to salvage something out of the encounter with the band. Maybe romance with the band members was out—*way* out—but there was still bound to be some fun and prestige. Jessica liked the idea of being associated with the band that was about to displace The Droids as the number-one act in Sweet Valley. That reminded her: She had no idea if Spontaneous Combustion was any good. She had never heard any of their songs!

For now, though, Jessica decided she had better pay attention to what Spy was saying about the various pieces of sound equipment that were scattered haphazardly around the basement.

"See this? And this here?" Spy spun a dial on an amp and pointed to an electric cord. "You've got to be careful or the whole thing will blow."

"And we definitely don't want any feedback," Wheels added.

"And, like, static is the enemy," Hal put in. "Understand, man, I mean, babe?"

"It's a lot to keep track of," Jessica said meekly.

"Oh, you can do it." Spy slung an arm around her, enveloping her in a cloud of cigarette smoke. "You've got ten days to get it straight. That's when we bury everyone at the battle of the bands."

Ten days! Jessica glanced at Lila, who was standing in between Pete and Wheels with her arms crossed.

Jessica had a feeling that those ten days were going to be the longest—and strangest—of their lives!

"Can we run through that song one more time?" Dana asked. She tipped her head to one side and studied Max Dellon, The Droids' lead guitarist. "And sing with me this time. The song feels like a duet to me."

Max picked out a blues riff on his electric guitar and grinned. "You really want me croaking on your song?"

"I want a male voice," Dana replied. "Yours is deeper than Dan's. I like that rough edge."

"You mean you think his voice is better than mine?" kidded Dan Scott, the bass guitarist, in a high falsetto.

Dana bounced away from the microphone to give Dan a playful slap. "C'mon, I'm serious, guys."

"Who are you calling a guy?" said petite Emily Mayer, the drummer, pretending to be indignant.

"This is what I want." Dana put her hands on Max's broad shoulders. "Just come in when you feel like it, nice and low. Just support me. Warm it up."

"OK, chief."

Dana grabbed the mike and hopped up and down a couple of times. "Let it rip!"

The Larsons' garage was instantly filled with hard, happy, pulsing sounds. Dana began belting out the lyrics she and the band had collaborated on earlier that afternoon. She sang with her whole heart, and her whole body. It had been a long time since singing had made her feel so good.

The rest of the band was just as pumped up as Dana was. Max and Guy Chesney, The Droids' keyboardist, ended the song with an impromptu guitar-keyboard jam. Dana stamped her feet and clapped her hands, urging them on. When they had worn themselves out, she threw her arms around Max in an exuberant hug. "I think we're ready!"

"Battle of the bands, here we come," Dan declared as he unplugged his bass. "And here I go. That's it for practice, isn't it?"

Dana nodded. "I'm drained. And my parents are going to be home from work any minute now. They might appreciate being able to put their cars in the garage."

It didn't take long to pack up the instruments and equipment. Sitting on a stepladder, an acoustic guitar resting on her thighs, Dana watched the others prepare to leave.

"How about a bite to eat?" Emily asked Dana. "I could go for pizza."

"No, thanks. You guys go ahead," Dana answered. "I'm still feeling kind of inspired. If I break now, I'll lose it."

"Great practice, Dana. You were on fire,"

said Max as he ducked out the side door of the garage.

"Hold onto that good mood," said Dan.

"If I didn't know you better, I'd say you were in love or something," Guy joked over his shoulder. Then the door closed behind them.

In love . . . If I didn't know myself better, I'd think the same thing, Dana mused. She strummed the guitar thoughtfully as another new song came to her.

Whatever happened to those sad, sarcastic songs? she wondered. What about "Fed Up with Love"? The music that had come out of Dana that afternoon had been full of joy and optimism. Dana was her old self again—maybe even better than her old self.

It's Aaron, Dana knew as she hummed one of The Droids' new love songs. She couldn't hide from her feelings any longer.

Maybe it was time to come out and tell the world—and most importantly, Aaron—that she wanted to take back all the bad things she had said about love.

She was ready to give it one more chance.

Eight

Dana was still flying high. It was Friday, one week before the battle of the bands, and a new set of colorful posters advertising the contest had been put up all over the halls. More and more people were coming up to Dana, asking her if The Droids were ready and wishing her luck. The battle of the bands wasn't what was on her mind at the moment, though. She was too busy anticipating the coming evening.

There was a new play at the Sweet Valley Civic Center, and when Elizabeth had called the night before suggesting that the two of them go with Todd and Aaron, Dana had jumped at the idea. It was another chance to be with Aaron, and this time Dana knew something had to happen between them.

Dana had just left the cafeteria. Now she checked her watch. There were ten minutes until her next class; she had time to stop by her locker.

Elizabeth was at her own locker farther down the hall. "Just who I wanted to see!" she called to Dana.

"Hi, Liz! What's up?"

Elizabeth waved an envelope in the air. "The tickets for tonight," she explained. "I just ran over to the Civic Center to buy them. The play's gotten a lot of good reviews, and I didn't want to risk just showing up and not getting seats."

"Great! But I'll have to pay you later," said Dana. "I don't have enough money on me."

"That's fine. Here." Elizabeth removed the two tickets from the envelope. "Why don't you hold on to these?" she suggested.

"Aren't we all driving over together?" Dana asked.

"Didn't Aaron mention it to you yet?" Elizabeth smiled. "He told me this morning that he'd pick you up himself tonight, and he hinted that he expected Todd and me to find our own way to the Civic Center!"

Dana couldn't keep from smiling. That news

really made her day! Aaron had to be thinking along the same lines that she was.

Dana spun the dial on her locker. "I can't wait," she said to Elizabeth. "I mean, for the play."

Elizabeth laughed. "I think I know what you mean."

Dana tugged on her locker. "This stupid thing is stuck. Oh, there it goes. What's this?"

Something had been wedged into her locker, and it fell to the floor. Dana picked up a slightly wrinkled envelope with her name written on it. "Somebody's sending me mail," she said. "I wonder who."

After tearing open the envelope, Dana pulled out a card. On the front was a misty, romantic scene with a boy and a girl walking hand in hand on a beach at sunset. Dana was about to laugh, thinking it must be a joke. Then she opened it and read the handwritten verse inside. "Roses are red, violets are blue, I've changed my mind, how about you?"

"Who's it from?" asked Elizabeth.

"It's not signed, but . . ." Dana was suddenly breathless. "It's from Aaron, I just know it! Liz, I have a confession to make." She smiled sheepishly. "Ever since he and I started spending time together, it seems like my life has turned around. That we're-just-friends stuff was only an act. I can't stop thinking about him!"

"I knew it!" Elizabeth declared happily. "Dana, I think you two make a terrific couple."

"So do I," said Dana, her eyes glowing. "And now that I know Aaron likes me, too, I'm going to tell him just how I feel when we go out tonight."

Elizabeth shook her head. "Who'd have thought it—Aaron Dallas, a romantic! Sending anonymous love notes." Dana held out the card, and Elizabeth skimmed the contents. "That's really sweet," she said.

Elizabeth started to close the card, but then she stopped and read the message again. When she looked up at Dana, her eyes were wide with surprise.

"Mushy, huh?" said Dana, taking the card and putting it in her shoulder bag.

"Yeah a little," Elizabeth said slowly. "You know, Dana—maybe it's not such a good idea to rush things."

"What do you mean?" Dana shut her locker.

"I mean, about tonight. Maybe you shouldn't come right out and tell Aaron the way you feel about him."

"Why not?" Dana asked. "I like him and he

likes me. In my opinion, it's time we were both honest about it."

"Well, maybe you should let him bring it up first," Elizabeth recommended. "Some guys get scared off if a girl comes on too strong."

Dana shook her head. "I don't believe that. The way I see it, any boy who'd get scared off by the truth isn't worth it. Anyway, Aaron's the one who sent *me* the card! *He* brought it up first."

"Still . . ."

"Aaron's asking me a question," Dana continued. " 'I've changed my mind, how about you?' I want to give him an answer."

"Maybe he is and maybe you do," Elizabeth conceded. "But if I were you, I wouldn't mention the card. It's the kind of thing Aaron might feel a little shy about. He's not as bold as you are, you know? That's why he wrote an anonymous note in the first place."

Dana considered. Maybe Elizabeth was right. After all, she did know Aaron better than Dana did. "OK, I won't say anything about the card. But I can't keep my feelings for him a secret! Don't worry," Dana assured her friend. "It's going to work out between Aaron and me. Tonight's going to be our night!"

Elizabeth smiled. "I hope so!

*　　*　　*

After leaving Dana at her locker, Elizabeth headed for the cafeteria, where she expected to find Todd. Sure enough, he was spending the last few minutes of lunch with a few of his friends, including Aaron.

Elizabeth stormed up to their table. Yanking on Todd's arm, she pulled him to his feet. "I have to talk to you," she whispered fiercely.

Todd looked startled. "OK, OK," he agreed. "Don't kill me!"

"Why on earth did you send that card to Dana?" Elizabeth demanded as soon as they were out of earshot of Aaron and the others.

"Oh, the card. How'd you find out about it?" Todd asked innocently.

"I was with Dana when she opened it, and I recognized your handwriting. Todd, how could you! You're going to ruin everything! She thinks Aaron sent it!"

"That's the whole point," explained Todd. "It's obvious Dana and Aaron have been growing closer lately, but it seemed to me like they'd reached a stalemate. I just wanted to help things along."

Elizabeth shook her head in disbelief. "Why didn't you ask me first?"

Todd shrugged. "It was kind of a spontane-ous thing. It didn't seem like such a big deal to me."

"Well, it will be a big deal if Dana mentions that card! And if either of them finds out about everything we've been doing . . ." Elizabeth said.

Todd looked crestfallen. "I guess I didn't think it through. I'm sorry, Liz."

Elizabeth sighed. "Oh, it's all right." She let Todd put his arm around her. Inside, though, she was still angry. She couldn't help suspect-ing that Todd was deliberately trying to mess up Aaron and Dana's relationship so he would win the bet. But he couldn't be that mean . . . could he? Elizabeth stared up at Todd, wishing she could read his mind. Was he up to some-thing, or had he really meant to help?

She would just have to make sure everything went smoothly between Aaron and Dana when they all went out that night. She had to see to it that Dana didn't go back to being fed up with love!

Dana had just stepped out of the shower that evening when the phone rang. She hurried down the hall and picked up the extension in her bedroom.

"Hi, Dana. This is Liz."

"Hi! What's up?" Dana replied cheerfully.

"I have some bad news," Elizabeth said. "Todd and I aren't going to make it to the play tonight."

"Oh, no!" Dana sat down on the edge of her bed. "What's wrong?"

"Well, you know I sometimes baby-sit for Mr. Collins's son, Teddy, right? Well, Mr. Collins had to go to L.A. on short notice. I think his father isn't feeling well. He couldn't find a baby-sitter for Teddy. All of the people he uses regularly were busy. So . . ."

"He called you, and of course you agreed to do it," Dana said.

"I had to," Elizabeth said. "He really needed my help. He's going to drop Teddy off at my house, and Todd said he'd keep me company."

"It's too bad you're going to miss the play. I know you were really looking forward to it," Dana said.

"Todd and I will probably end up watching cartoons with Teddy instead!" Elizabeth laughed. "Just make sure you take notes, so you can let me know what I missed."

"I'll tell you all about it," Dana promised.

"I hope you and Aaron have fun. I have to run. I'll talk to you tomorrow, OK?"

"Sure thing," Dana said. "Talk to you later, then!"

She hung up the phone. Trust Elizabeth to give up her Friday night to help someone. Dana hoped Mr. Collins's father was all right.

She dropped the bath towel over the back of her desk chair and slipped into her terry cloth robe. It was a shame that Elizabeth and Todd wouldn't be able to make it to the play. But at the same time . . . Dana certainly didn't mind going out alone with Aaron! It would be like their first real date.

Dana saw that Aaron had the same response she did when he picked her up forty-five minutes later. He didn't seem to mind at all that Todd and Elizabeth weren't going to meet them later—in fact, he seemed almost happy about it. The electricity fairly crackled between him and Dana as they drove to the Civic Center.

They found their seats in the auditorium and had time to read their programs and take a look around before the play started. As the lights dimmed and the curtain rose, Dana thought she had never felt so alive. She had found other boys exciting in the past, but usually it seemed that the better she got to know them, the less appealing they turned out to be. The opposite had been true with Aaron. The more she saw of him, the more she saw to like in him. And soon she would be able to tell him how she felt about him.

The first act of the play was fast paced and funny. Dana expected Aaron's nearness to distract her, but instead, all her senses seemed to be heightened. She never stopped being aware of his arm touching hers, his warmth when he bent over to whisper something in her ear, but the play made an impression on her, too. The characters struck her as exceptionally real. One character in particular, a woman who was disillusioned with love, reminded Dana of herself—or rather, herself before she got to know Aaron.

At intermission Dana and Aaron pushed their way out into the lobby with the rest of the audience. Aaron waited in line for five minutes for soft drinks and then rejoined Dana in a corner of the lobby. The room was packed, so they were forced to stand very close together. Dana wasn't about to complain.

"Isn't the play great?" she said. "It's funny the way theater works. I can't wait to find out what's going to happen to these people. I mean, I care about them as if they were my friends!"

"I know what you mean. I can see why the play's such a hit. I'm totally caught up in what's her name—Abby's—situation," Aaron commented.

Dana nodded. Abby was the woman who was disillusioned with love. "I think she's going to realize that that guy who's been her best friend forever, Louis, is really meant to be her true love."

"So do I," said Aaron.

"At least, that's what I'm hoping," Dana added meaningfully.

Aaron stared into her eyes. "Me, too."

Dana took a quick sip of her drink. *That's my cue*, she thought, suddenly nervous. *This is my chance.*

"Um, Aaron," she began.

Just then, the lights dimmed, indicating that it was time to return to their seats. Dana was both disappointed and relieved.

"Were you going to say something?" Aaron asked as he ushered her back into the theater.

"Nothing that can't wait," Dana replied. But she didn't want to wait too much longer!

Dana enjoyed the second act just as much as the first, and she was happy that the play ended just as she had predicted, with Abby and Louis finally discovering their love for each other. It was a good omen, Dana decided. It was going to be a night for happy endings, she just knew it.

If only the evening didn't have to end so soon! Dana wished the play had gone on longer. Well, there was always the car ride back to her house. She would have to find a way to bring up the subject of their relationship then.

In the parking lot behind the Civic Center Aaron paused with his hand on the car door on the passenger side.

He looked at Dana hopefully. "What do you say, Dana, can I keep you out a little longer? How about dessert at the Box Tree Café?"

Can you keep me out a little longer—are you kidding? Dana thought, thrilled. And the Box Tree Café was a wonderfully romantic little restaurant. "That sounds great," she answered. At the café she would finally be able to tell Aaron just how she felt about him.

Fifteen minutes later they were seated at a secluded table for two by one of the tall windows. The candle on the table flickered, casting shadows on their faces. Still, Aaron's eyes seemed to be sparkling in the dim light. He looked even more gorgeous than usual.

Dana gazed across the table at him. For a long time, neither one of them said anything. Dana didn't want to ruin the magic of the moment. She was so happy it almost hurt. Forget everything she had ever said about not wanting to fall in love. This dizzy, exciting feeling was exactly what she wanted!

"There's something I have to tell you," Aaron began, looking deep into her eyes.

"You don't have to," Dana said softly. She put her hand on top of his. "Your card said it all."

"My card?" Aaron repeated, looking puzzled.

"The card you put in my locker this morning." Dana smiled. "It was such a romantic thing to do."

Aaron stared at her blankly, and Dana's heart sank. He seemed to have absolutely no idea what she was talking about!

Dana looked down at the unopened menu, wondering what she should say next. Maybe Elizabeth had been right after all. Maybe Aaron was embarrassed about sending the card.

But she had to know the truth. She had to know if he really cared. It was time for them to be honest with each other.

Dana put her hand in her purse. She had

brought the card along. Now she pulled it out and put it on the table. "Don't be embarrassed," she told Aaron. "Really. I was happy when I read it."

Aaron's eyebrows shot up. "Dana, I didn't send you any card." He opened it. "This isn't even my handwriting!"

Dana stared at him. She could feel a hot blush spreading across her face. The magic had been destroyed, and an awkward silence had taken its place. Dana wished she could turn back the clock and keep her mouth shut. Why did she have to mention that stupid card? And if Aaron hadn't sent her the card, who had—and why?

Dana reached for the card, planning to stuff it back into her purse. She wanted it out of her sight as quickly as possible.

"Wait a minute." Aaron put his hand on hers. "Let me see that again." He took another look at the card. His eyebrows rose once more. "That's Todd's handwriting!" he exclaimed, astonished.

Dana gaped at him. "Todd's?"

Aaron nodded. "I'd know it anywhere."

"But why would Todd send me a card like this?" Dana asked.

Aaron shook his head. "Beats me."

Dana stared at the card lying on the table. What was going on? Had Todd lost his mind, or was this just a practical joke on her and Aaron? Suddenly, as she stared at the romantic couple on the card, the pieces of a very disturbing puzzle came together in Dana's mind. Suddenly, she saw the wonderful events of the last week in a new, terrible light.

Elizabeth telling her not to mention the card to Aaron; all the times Elizabeth and Todd told her how much Aaron liked her, even when Dana herself couldn't believe it was true; the initial setup when Aaron had gone to the movies with them. In an instant, Dana realized that Todd and Elizabeth had decided Aaron liked her. Aaron didn't have anything to do with it!

Dana was trembling. Now as she met Aaron's uncomprehending gaze, she felt both ashamed and betrayed. He didn't really like her. He was just a friend, after all. Elizabeth and Todd tried to get her to like Aaron, and they had succeeded. They had made a complete fool out of her!

She had opened herself up, taken a chance on a new guy—and it was all a big joke!

"Dana, whatever the story is behind the card, I—"

Dana couldn't bear to hear Aaron's voice. She

had never felt so exposed. She couldn't spend another instant with Aaron, knowing that he didn't return her affection.

Not waiting for Aaron to finish his sentence, Dana jumped up from her chair and ran out of the café.

Nine

"This is just the way I wanted to spend my Friday night," Lila muttered. She lifted an amplifier and groaned loudly.

"Well, don't blame me," Jessica said as she pushed another amplifier toward the space Spy had indicated. "I didn't force you to be a roadie."

"Yeah, but you tricked me into thinking it was going to be fun! I've broken three fingernails already." Moaning, Lila dropped the amp where she stood. "And I can't carry this thing another inch!"

"Well, I guess you'll just have to make an emergency appointment with your manicurist!" Jessica snapped. "Here, I'll do that," she said through gritted teeth. Bending at the waist, she shoved the amplifier a few more feet.

"Good enough," Motor said, nodding. "You know, you chicks do pretty good work."

Jessica raised an eyebrow. If they referred to her as chick one more time, she was going to scream.

"String!" Hal shouted.

Jessica glanced at Lila. It was Lila's turn to replace a broken guitar string; Jessica had already done two that evening.

But Lila ignored both Hal and Jessica. Instead, she sat down on top of an amp and began filing one of her damaged nails.

Heaving a put-upon sigh, Jessica walked over to Hal. She handed him his backup guitar and took the other in order to repair it. "Thanks, chicklet," he said, laughing at his own joke.

Jessica felt a scream beginning in her throat. She didn't get a chance to scream, though. Pete did it for her—he started singing!

Jessica clapped her hands over her ears and joined Lila in the corner of the community hall rec room the band had reserved for a "dress rehearsal." There was no getting away from Spontaneous Combustion, however. Jessica had a feeling she would probably still be able to hear them if she was at home in her room.

"That's not music, that's noise pollution!" Lila shouted.

"Tell me about it!" Jessica shouted back.

"I don't know how much more of this I can take," Lila complained. "What good will it be to go to L.A. and meet Jamie Peters if we can't hear what he says to us?"

Jessica didn't get a chance to respond. Wheels was gesturing frantically to her with a broken drumstick. She had to get him a new one fast; there was a big drum solo at the end of this hideous song. What was the song called—"Hold Me Till I Hate You"? Something disgusting like that.

After delivering the drumstick, Jessica collapsed on a pile of the canvas tarpaulins that were used to cover and secure the equipment when it was inside the group's van. She knew she should conserve her energy. After the band finished jamming, she and Lila would have to load all the equipment back into the van for the return trip to Spy's house. Scratch that; *she* would have to load all the equipment. Lila, the world's laziest, most spoiled person, was basically useless. Jessica had been bearing the brunt of the sweaty, grubby work from the beginning.

And I thought rock 'n' roll was going to be glamorous! Jessica thought as Spontaneous Combustion launched into an ear-splitting rendition of

"Just Call Me Mr. Zero." Spy had been right on target when he wrote that song! Only, Jessica thought she could call him a few more things, too: Mr. Rude, Ugly, and Untalented!

At eleven o'clock Elizabeth and Todd were watching television in the Wakefields' den. Mr. Collins had come to pick Teddy up at around ten-thirty. His father was fine—it was just a bad case of the flu. Elizabeth had enjoyed spending the evening with Teddy. He was a cute kid, and Todd was great about playing with him, too.

Elizabeth was sitting with her head comfortably nestled in the crook of Todd's shoulder. When the phone rang, she sat bolt upright.

She stretched to reach the phone on the end table. "Hello?" she said.

"Is this Liz?" an irate female voice demanded.

"Yes. Dana, is that you? How was the—"

Dana cut Elizabeth off. "The play was fine, a lot better than my *life*, thanks to you and Todd!"

"What?" Elizabeth blinked. "Dana, what's wrong?"

"As if you need to ask!" Dana cried. "I'm

calling to tell you that I've figured out your little scheme. I don't know why you and Todd have been trying to get Aaron and me together, but you can forget about it. After tonight, I'm sure he'll never want to see me again, and I feel the same way!"

"Dana, calm down," Elizabeth begged. "Tell me what happened. Maybe I can explain—"

"I don't want to hear any more of your lies!" Dana's voice was shaking with emotion. "My friendship with Aaron is over, and my friendship with you is over, too!" With that, Dana slammed the phone down so hard that it made Elizabeth's ear ring.

In a state of bewilderment, Elizabeth replaced the receiver. What on earth had gone wrong for Dana and Aaron? How had Dana discovered that Elizabeth and Todd had been trying to get them together?

Then Elizabeth remembered the card that Todd had put in Dana's locker.

She turned to face Todd on the couch, her eyes suddenly ablaze with anger. "Are you satisfied now?" she demanded. "Are you happy that you've ruined Dana and Aaron's chance for happiness? That's what you wanted, wasn't it?"

"Huh?" Todd said in surprise.

"Don't 'huh' me!" Elizabeth cried. "You know exactly what I'm talking about! You deliberately sabotaged my plan to match up Aaron and Dana by sending that card. That was the stupidest thing you've ever done!"

Todd sat up straighter. "You think that card was stupid, Liz? I'll tell you what's stupid. Your matchmaking idea was stupid. Stupid from the very start!"

"It was not! It was working fine until you messed it up. You just had to win our bet, didn't you? How could you be so selfish!"

"You're calling *me* selfish?" Todd said in disbelief. "You're the one who can't even see beyond your own nose! Whatever put it in your head to try to fix up Aaron and Dana, I'll never understand."

"*You* put it in my head!" Elizabeth reminded him. "Admit it, it wasn't such a crazy idea. And I'm not the one who's in the wrong—you are!"

"I sent that card in good faith," Todd insisted.

"Yeah, in good faith that it would split Dana and Aaron up for good!"

"That's it!" Todd jumped up from the couch. "I'm not going to try to reason with you!"

Elizabeth shot him a withering glance.

"Yeah, why bother talking to me? Why don't you just write me an anonymous *note*?"

Todd didn't reply. He gave her one last furious look, then grabbed his jacket and stormed into the hall. Elizabeth followed him. Flinging the front door open, Todd stomped out of the house and down the walk to the driveway without once looking back. Elizabeth slammed the door with all her might behind him.

Turning around, she rested her back against the door and squeezed her eyes shut. She was so upset, she could hear her heart pounding. Todd was so bullheaded! Why couldn't he admit he'd made a big mistake?

At that moment, Elizabeth felt someone push on the door. She stepped back, and it swung open slowly.

Jessica walked slowly past Elizabeth into the front hall without saying a word. Her face was smudged with dirt, her hair was in disarray, and she was walking with a noticeable limp.

"What happened to *you*?" Elizabeth asked, concerned. "You look like you got hit by a truck!"

Jessica's eyes flashed with irritation. "Well, if I do, it's all your fault!"

"My fault?" Elizabeth didn't understand.

Jessica started slowly up the stairs. "Yes,"

113

she muttered. "If you hadn't fixed dumb Dana Larson up with dumb Aaron Dallas . . ." Her voice trailed off as she disappeared upstairs. Then there was a loud *bang* as Jessica slammed her bedroom door.

Elizabeth stared after her sister. Jessica was mad at her, too? What was going on?

All Elizabeth knew was that she had started off trying to make two people happy, and now she had the whole world—Dana, Todd, even her sister—mad at her. Where had she gone wrong?

Ten

"What'll it be?" Mr. Wakefield asked his daughter. "Belgian waffles, eggs to order—you name it, I'll serve it."

Elizabeth laughed as her handsome father struck a chef's pose by the stove. "Playing short-order cook, Dad? I can't resist—I'll try some of those waffles."

"You won't be sorry," he promised.

"No, but I may have to swim a few extra laps in the pool later as penance!"

Mrs. Wakefield was halving oranges for fresh-squeezed orange juice. Elizabeth joined her at the counter. Sunday brunch had always been a family tradition, and it made Elizabeth happy to see her parents engaged in the familiar routine. Only a short time ago, the Wakefield home had been in painful upheaval. The twins' parents had separated for a brief time, during which Elizabeth was afraid her family would never be whole again. Since Mr. and Mrs. Wakefield had reconciled their differences, their marriage was stronger than ever.

The atmosphere in the kitchen was warm and relaxed—until Jessica shuffled in a minute later.

"You're up early, honey," Mrs. Wakefield observed. "I thought after your late rehearsal with the band, you'd sleep until noon at least."

Jessica yawned. "I could hardly fall asleep at all last night, my ears were ringing so badly," she said crabbily. "Then I had nightmares. I dreamed I wasn't just doing one show with Spontaneous Combustion—I had to tour all over the country with them! It was awful."

Elizabeth couldn't help giggling. Jessica shot her a poisonous look. Mrs. Wakefield intercepted it.

Elizabeth knew her mother had picked up on the fact that her daughters weren't speaking to each other—or rather, that, since Friday night, Jessica wasn't speaking to Elizabeth.

"Why don't you two set the table on the patio?" Mrs. Wakefield suggested. "Your father and I will take care of breakfast."

Elizabeth counted out silverware and paper

apkins; Jessica hoisted a stack of plates. The wo walked out to the patio in silence.

Jessica deposited the plates. She was about o return to the kitchen without having spoken o or even looked at her twin, when Elizabeth uddenly threw the napkins down on the table.

"Jess, you can't still be mad at me!" Elizabeth ried in frustration. "I don't even know why ou are."

Jessica saw the tears sparkling in Elizabeth's yes. Her grouchy expression faded, remorse aking its place. "Liz, I'm not really mad at ou," she confessed. "I'm sorry I snapped at ou the other night. It's just been a bad week. ut what's got you so upset? It can't just be he."

Elizabeth pulled out a chair; Jessica did the ame. "Remember my plan to fix up Aaron and Dana? Operation Pair-Up?"

Jessica grimaced. "Do I ever."

"Well, it bombed in a major way. I don't now exactly how, but Dana found out about , and she and Aaron must have had some ind of argument on Friday night. Then she nd *I* had an argument. Then *Todd* and I had n argument. Then *you* and I had an argument, r at least you yelled at me!"

Jessica had to laugh. "Poor Liz! You couldn't

117

even yell back because you didn't know wha my problem was!" She leaned forward an gave Elizabeth a hug.

"Well, while we're on the subject, you migh as well clue me in," said Elizabeth. "I knov why Dana and Todd are mad at me. What' your reason?"

Jessica's nose wrinkled. "It's this whol roadie thing," she explained. "See, I was kin of ticked off when you decided to get Dan together with Aaron. I thought it would serv Dana right if The Droids were beaten in th battle of the bands. Plus I liked the idea of win ning a trip to L.A. to meet celebrities and tha sort of thing. That's why I hooked up witl Spontaneous Combustion."

"And it's not working out the way yo thought?" Elizabeth guessed.

Jessica groaned. "*I'm* working, but it's no Liz, every muscle in my body aches. I have t shampoo my hair three times after every prac tice to get the smell of cigarette smoke out c it. And Lila never lifts a finger. I'm the one wh has to jump every time Spy or Motor or Wheel wants something!"

"Spy or Motor or Wheels. . . ?" Elizabetl doubled over with laughter. "Jess, you're no really working for people named Motor and Wheels!"

"Yes, I am," said Jessica, "and it's not funny. That bad dream I had wasn't any worse than what's happening in real life. Last night Wheels had the nerve to ask me if I wanted to be his chick!"

Elizabeth was laughing so hard she could barely breathe. "His . . . *chick?*"

Jessica's lips twitched. Soon she was laughing, too. "I informed him that Jessica Wakefield wasn't anybody's chick," she told Elizabeth, between giggles. "Then I poked him in his wimpy chest, hard, with one of his stupid drumsticks. I think he got the message."

Elizabeth sank back in her chair weakly. "Good for you! I only wish I was as successful in my attempts at communicating with people these days."

"Well, maybe you've learned a lesson," Jessica observed. "Maybe you should get out of the matchmaking business before anything else goes wrong. Unless of course the match you're making is between a gorgeous guy and me," she added.

"I think you're right," Elizabeth agreed. She had learned her lesson, and she had learned it the hard way. Never again would she interfere in someone else's affairs, even if it was with the best of intentions.

At that moment, Mr. Wakefield appeared with a platter of steaming waffles. Mrs. Wakefield followed, carrying a pitcher of orange juice.

"I'm starved!" Jessica exclaimed, her mood suddenly improved. "Dad, those smell divine."

As the four settled around the table for brunch, Elizabeth felt a rush of gratitude. She was lucky to be part of such a wonderful, loving family. If only it were going to be as easy to make up with Dana as it had been with Jessica. As for Todd . . . Elizabeth wasn't sure things would ever be the same between them.

Dana was already out of her chair by the time the bell stopped ringing. She managed to beat the rest of her history class to the door by two long strides.

It was Monday, three days after Dana's disastrous date with Aaron and her fight with Elizabeth. History was the only class Dana and Elizabeth had together. Dana knew that Elizabeth was trying to get her attention. She had already stopped her once at her locker and once in the hallway. Both times, Dana had breezed by her as if she didn't see her.

Now as she stepped into the bustling hallway, she heard Elizabeth call her name. Dana didn't look back. This time, however, Elizabeth didn't accept the brush-off. She put her hand on Dana's arm. "Dana, please. I have to talk to you."

Dana froze. Turning slowly, she faced Elizabeth, willing herself to remain cold and calm.

It was hard when she saw Elizabeth's sad eyes and anxious expression. A needle of guilt stabbed Dana's heart. Then the guilt changed into anger. *Why should I feel guilty?* Dana thought. *She's the one who humiliated me!*

Dana lifted her chin. She didn't speak.

"I'm sorry, Dana." Elizabeth spoke quickly, as if she were trying to squeeze the words in before Dana turned her back on her again. "I know I made a mistake, but you have to believe that I never meant for things to turn out this way. I only wanted—"

Dana had heard enough. "Apologies are useless. The damage is already done," she said in a chilly tone. With one final glare at Elizabeth, Dana spun on her heel and walked away. This time, Elizabeth let her go.

Dana kept her shoulders straight and her face

expressionless all the way to the nearest girls' rest room. Once inside, she began to crumble. *I should have just stayed home sick today*, Dana thought. After all, she *was* sick—sick at heart. And it was such an effort to pretend that nothing was wrong when she was sure that all of Sweet Valley High was whispering about her. How many people had known about Elizabeth and Todd's little scheme? How many people were changing their opinion of Dana Larson from "cool" to "fool"?

As she stared at her reflection in the mirror, a tear slid down Dana's cheek. She grabbed a paper towel and dabbed at the tear, but soon another fell . . . and another, and another.

The embarrassment wasn't really what was bothering Dana. What hurt so much was the pain deep inside her—the pain of losing Aaron. Dana had always thought it was the kind of thing that only happened in corny love songs, but now she knew differently.

Dana blew her nose and quickly washed her face. She checked the mirror again. Her eyes looked like those of a sad puppy, she thought, and her mouth seemed to be set in a permanent frown. Dana sighed. She could hardly wait for the school day to be over. She could lose herself, and her hurt and disappointment, in a practice session with The Droids. *Life goes on,* she reminded herself, attempting to be philosophical. *The music keeps playing.*

Dana took a deep breath and walked out of the rest room, prepared to face the world once more. She turned a corner in the hallway—and collided with Aaron.

Dana's books started to slip from her grasp. Aaron gripped her arm to steady her. At his touch, Dana felt tears threaten again.

"Dana, I called you ten times yesterday!" Aaron exclaimed. "Didn't you get my messages?"

Dana's face turned scarlet. "No . . . well, yes, but—"

"What happened the other night?" he continued. "You left the café in such a rush—I was really worried! How did you get home?"

"A cab." Dana took a step backward, and Aaron was forced to drop his hand from her arm.

He frowned. "Dana, I think we need to talk," he said quietly.

"Some other time," Dana said, her voice shaking. "I—I have to go."

"But Dana, I . . ."

Aaron's voice faded behind Dana as she bolted into the crowd of students moving down the corridor. Her heart was pounding so rapidly, she thought it might burst. Seeing Aaron . . . his touch. . . . But it had only been a friendly touch, Dana reminded herself. Unfortunately, the racing of her heart told Dana that her feelings hadn't changed one bit since the incident at the Box Tree Café. She had fallen in love with Aaron Dallas, and she couldn't fall back out now.

After history on Tuesday and again on Wednesday, Elizabeth didn't even try to catch up with Dana. Dana was out the door before Elizabeth closed her notebook and capped her pen. She had phoned her at home several times, too, but Dana hadn't returned her calls. Elizabeth sighed heavily. It looked as if her friendship with Dana was history, too.

There was someone else who always hurried out of history class as soon as the bell rang— Claire Middleton. Elizabeth had been meaning to have a word with Claire to see if she could break through the new girl's shyness. Today, however, she just didn't feel up to the effort. All her thoughts were on Aaron and Dana.

Why did I ever try to get them together? Elizabeth wondered as she walked in the direction of her locker. *Why did I have to meddle?*

She had thought it would be harmless; so had everyone else. What was the worst that could happen? Elizabeth remembered asking herself and her friends. At the time, she imagined the worst was simply that Operation Pair-Up wouldn't work. She never expected it to backfire so drastically. She hadn't anticipated hurt feelings.

Elizabeth approached her locker. Then her heart jumped. Coming her way down the hall was Todd. *He came to find me. He wants to apologize!*

Elizabeth hadn't spoken to Todd, or seen him except in passing, since their fight on Friday night. He hadn't called, and she was afraid to call him. In the heat of the moment, she had blamed him completely for the Dana–Aaron disaster. But later, Elizabeth had started to wonder if perhaps she'd been unfair. Maybe Todd *had* just meant to help when he sent the card to Dana.

Elizabeth wasn't sure anymore who was right and who was wrong. She only knew she didn't like being mad at Todd. If he was willing to take the first step like this, she would meet him halfway.

A smile brightened Elizabeth's face. She opened her mouth, ready to echo Todd's greeting. He walked right by her, not even giving her a glance.

He wasn't waiting for her, Elizabeth realized, disappointed. He was just on his way to his next class like everyone else in the hallway.

Slowly, anger replaced hurt. Elizabeth glared at Todd's retreating figure. If he wanted to hold this grudge forever, she'd be happy to oblige him!

"Let's get with it! We only have two more days," Dana reminded the rest of The Droids. Once again, the band had failed to get the harmony right on a song they'd had down cold a week ago.

Dana knew it was her own fault. She was the one who couldn't seem to hit any of the right notes. Her voice was off because her heart was off.

Guy ran his hand over the keyboards. "Maybe we should call it a day," he suggested. "We'll have more to put into our final practice that way."

Max had already unstrapped his guitar. "I'm outta here," he informed the others.

Emily covered her drum set, then crossed the garage to Dana's side. She put an arm around Dana's shoulders. "Just get a good night's sleep," she advised. "Everything will come together tomorrow. We still have time."

"Thanks, Em," Dana said. There was something comforting about spending time with The Droids. They moved in different circles at school, and she was pretty sure they didn't know anything about the Aaron Dallas episode. *She* certainly hadn't mentioned it.

Left alone in the garage, Dana wandered over to a cardboard box in the corner. Inside were the costumes DeeDee and Olivia had made for The Droids to wear in the battle of the bands. The two girls had dropped them off earlier in the afternoon.

Dana lifted out the shirt she would wear for the contest. It was a wild tiger print, low cut and sleekly fitting. It would look great with her black leather pants.

Dana tossed the shirt back into the box, wishing she could care about how she was going to look and sound when The Droids performed on Friday night. She knew DeeDee and Olivia had worked hard on the costumes. The band had been working hard, too, and they deserved to win.

Somehow Dana had to get herself psyched to appear onstage in front of the entire Sweet Valley High student body. She couldn't just go through the motions, and she couldn't let The Droids down. For the first time, it occurred to Dana that The Droids might lose. She knew that if they did, it would be all her fault. *I wish I'd never met Aaron*, Dana thought.

There was one thing she knew for sure: The battle of the bands was going to be the toughest gig she had ever played.

Eleven

Jessica didn't think she had ever seen the gym in such an uproar. The battle of the bands wasn't going to start for another forty-five minutes, but already several hundred students were staking out the best seats on the floor and in the bleachers. In the middle of the gym, a huge stage had been erected, and the four bands were scurrying frantically as they set up and checked their equipment. Each band had one corner of the stage. The spotlight would shift from band to band, starting with the Suede Men, who were up first.

"Get a move on it, chick!"

Jessica glanced up from the amp she was adjusting. "Are you talking to me?" she asked Spy with more than a touch of sarcasm.

"I want those microphone stands in place, pronto!"

"Aye-aye, captain!" One by one Jessica hauled the stands up onto the stage, muttering under her breath the whole time. It hadn't taken her long to discover that being a roadie was especially difficult in a miniskirt. Spy had told her and Lila to dress all in black for the big event, to match the band's outfits. Jessica didn't want to look anything like the guys in the band! But, keeping in mind the fact that all of Sweet Valley High would see her helping out Spontaneous Combustion onstage, Jessica had worn a black mini and a cute cropped black top. Now she wished she had just worn jeans! Her stockings already had a run in them, and every time she bent over to lift something, she could feel the seams in her skirt straining. Knowing her luck, the skirt would probably split right in two when the spotlight was on her.

Jessica dropped one of the microphone stands on her foot. "Ouch!" She hopped up and down on the other foot. "Where's Lila, anyway?" she demanded. Jessica was going to strangle that girl. She was sick of getting stuck with all the grunt work!

As if on cue, Lila stepped onto the stage.

She's not wearing black! Jessica noted, surprised. Then she noticed something else suspicious. Lila's wrist looked very bulky—and it wasn't because of any jewelry!

Jessica bounded over to Lila, who was talking to Spy. She arrived just in time to catch the tail end of Lila's pathetic excuse. "It's a sprain," Lila whined, rubbing her bandaged wrist and wincing. "I can't do anything with it. I'm afraid I'm not going to be able to help you tonight, Spy."

Jessica couldn't believe her ears. What a crummy lie!

"I'm sure Jessica can manage on her own," Lila said, backing away from Spy. "Good luck. I really hope you win!" she said, giving him a phony smile.

"Fowler, you weasel!" Jessica shouted, hurrying after Lila. She was ready to rip the Ace Bandage right off and expose Lila for what she was—a big fake.

She was too late. With a smug backward glance at Jessica, Lila jumped off the stage and vanished into the crowd of music fans.

I'll kill her, Jessica swore to herself as she started arranging the band's bewildering array of amplifiers. Then she yelped. "Hey!" Someone had pinched her, right on the bottom!

Jessica whirled around. It was Wheels, who was wearing a black shirt with a white stripe up the middle. He looked like a pale, skinny skunk.

He grinned. "I just love chick roadies. Keep up the good work, chicklet!"

Jessica gritted her teeth. She was holding one of the electrical cords, and it was all she could do to restrain herself from strangling Wheels with it. There were too many people watching, she decided. So instead, she started plugging in the numerous amp cords and cables entirely at random. She didn't care whether she got it right or not. She certainly didn't care whether or not Spontaneous Combustion—more like Spontaneous *Slimeballs*, she thought—won the battle of the bands. All Jessica wanted to do was get through the night. Then she never wanted to see—*or hear*—Spontaneous Combustion again.

Dana had thought nothing could lift her spirits, but as The Droids set up onstage in the gym, she felt herself revving up. She even started smiling and dancing as she moved around the stage, checking the equipment. Grabbing Guy, she gave him a spontaneous hug. There was nothing she loved better than performing with The Droids. She had to be at her best if they were going to win, and she *would* be. She wasn't going to let the band—or its fans—down.

"Hey, Dana! Break a leg!"

Dana glanced up. Andy Jenkins was waving to her from Baja Beat's corner of the stage. She grinned and waved back. The rivalry between them was friendly. "Good luck! May the best band win!"

"Hey, Dana." This time the words came from behind her. The voice was low and familiar.

Dana turned slowly. Aaron was standing on the floor alongside the stage, looking up at her.

She stared at him, her heart in her throat. A week hadn't dimmed the intensity of Dana's feelings for Aaron, or lessened her embarrassment. She had continued to avoid him at school all week, but she was trapped. There was no place to run.

"I knew I'd find you here," Aaron began. "Dana, I have to talk to you." A ghost of a smile flickered across his face. "Please don't make me get up there and carry you off by force!"

Dana sat down on the edge of the stage, too surprised to protest. Aaron took her hand and

133

helped her down. "This place is a zoo," Dana commented nervously. The moment her feet hit the floor, she dropped Aaron's hand. "I mean, there's not exactly a lot of privacy."

"I know somewhere we can talk," Aaron assured her with another smile. "Follow me." He took Dana's hand again and this time held it tightly so that she couldn't let go.

They wove their way through the crowded gym. When they reached their destination, Dana burst out laughing. "The soccer field?"

Aaron nodded. "Shouldn't be anybody practicing a goal kick at this time of night! C'mon."

A minute later they were seated side by side on one of the benches on the bleachers. Dana looked down at her folded hands, waiting for Aaron to speak and preparing herself to reply calmly. She was fairly sure what he was planning to say. He would tell her that he just liked her as a friend, and she would say, "That's fine. I never wanted anything else, either. Let's just forget the other night ever happened." She'd be completely cool. She wouldn't let him see how much she was hurting.

"Dana, look at me."

Dana took a deep breath. Raising her eyes, she met Aaron's. His expression was serious, and if she hadn't known better, she would have thought it was loving, too. He was probably just feeling sorry for her, Dana thought, biting her lip.

"Dana, I know why you ran away from me at the café," Aaron said at last.

She raised her eyebrows. "You do?"

"Todd finally told me everything today. About how he and Elizabeth had been scheming to get you and me together, and that he sent the card so you'd think it was from me."

"I'm surprised he had the nerve to admit it!" Dana exclaimed.

"Well, he feels pretty bad about it," Aaron explained. "He realized he blew it with the card, and he wanted to make up for it. He and Liz got into a big fight about it— I guess they're still not talking. Anyway, Todd thought if he explained the whole situation to me, I'd be able to take it from there. And that's what I'm going to do."

Here it comes, Dana thought. Aaron was going to try to let her down easy. Little did he know she was already down about as low as a person could get. "I don't know why Todd and Liz didn't mind their own business!" Dana suddenly cried, unable to contain her misery any longer. She covered her face with her hands.

For a moment there was silence. Then Aaron

135

took Dana's hands in his and pulled them away from her face. She had no choice but to look at him. "I don't know why, either," Aaron said quietly. "And I'm still not sure why they wanted you and me to fall for each other. But you know what, Dana?"

All at once, Aaron's eyes were glowing just the way they had on Friday night in the candle-light, before Dana had shattered the mood by mentioning the card. "What?" she whispered.

"Their plan worked!" Aaron answered. "I thought I'd had it with romance and dating and all that stuff, but I changed my mind. And that's what I was going to tell you at the Box Tree Café. Dana, I'm crazy about you."

Dana's eyes widened. That was the last thing she had expected him to say! It was what she had been dreaming he would say to her ever since she discovered the depth of her own feel-ings. "I'm crazy about you, too," she confessed shyly.

Dana bent forward and Aaron did the same. Their lips met in a passionate, electric kiss.

After a long moment, they parted. Both had silly grins on their faces. "Look at us!" said Aaron. "The two people who swore they'd never have anything to do with love ever again!"

"Pretty hypocritical of us, huh?" Dana agreed cheerfully. "Not that I've changed my mind one hundred percent, mind you."

Aaron's smile faded. "You haven't?"

"I still think falling in love is stupid," Dana remarked, a mischievous sparkle in her eyes. "But who says you have to be smart all the time?"

Five minutes later Dana rose to her feet reluctantly. She would have been happy to have kissed Aaron all night long! But she had a feeling the band would never forgive her.

She and Aaron walked slowly, their arms around each other's waists. Dana was in a trance of happiness. She still couldn't believe this was happening.

At the door to the gym, Aaron gave her one more kiss. "For luck," he said.

She smiled. She'd already had her luck. She had Aaron! And it was thanks to Todd, Dana realized at that moment. Todd's conversation with Aaron had made the difference. Meanwhile, according to Aaron, Todd and Elizabeth were still not speaking to each other.

Aaron observed Dana's thoughtful frown. "I think I know what you're thinking," he said. "Todd and Liz?"

Dana nodded. "Now that we've gotten

together, there's one more thing we have to do."

"Two more," Aaron corrected her. "The Droids have to win the battle of the bands!"

"And you and I have to end the battle between Elizabeth and Todd!" Dana concluded.

When The Droids wrapped up their set, Jessica cheered at the top of her lungs, along with the rest of the students gathered in the gymnasium. She knew it was disloyal; she should be saving her voice to yell for Spontaneous Combustion. But Jessica couldn't help herself. The Droids had really blown the roof off! Dana had sung like Jessica had never heard her sing before. Jessica couldn't stop dancing as she scurried around helping Spy and the others make the final adjustments on their equipment.

There was no doubt about it, Jessica thought. So far the audience clearly preferred The Droids over Baja Beat and the Suede Men. The radio station deejays who were acting as judges had an obvious winner, unless Spontaneous Combustion could top The Droids' act.

Finally, it was their turn. Spy, Hal, Pete, Wheels, and Motor took their places onstage. The spotlight shifted, gleaming off the shiny electric guitars and the chrome of the drums. Jessica crossed her fingers. She really didn't think Spontaneous Combustion had a prayer of beating The Droids, but after all was said and done, maybe they weren't such a bad bunch of guys. And if by some chance they actually won the battle of the bands, Jessica decided the trip to L.A. would make up for all the misery she had suffered.

Just then, Jessica saw a couple of loose cables lying on the stage behind the band. Something wasn't plugged in, she realized—something wasn't going to work!

Bending over so the spotlight wouldn't catch her, Jessica scooted forward. After grabbing the two cables, she quickly plugged them into the nearest outlets on the back of a large amplifier. Everything was connected anyway, she figured. One outlet was probably as good as another.

An instant later Spy swung his arm in a wide, dramatic arc. Jessica knew the gesture. He was about to rip into the first lick on his electric guitar. Instinctively, she covered her ears.

Boom! Jessica pressed her hands even closer. What was that? Instead of deafening rock music, there was a flash of light and a small explosion.

As Jessica watched in horror, the smaller amplifiers that she had just wired to the big one shorted out. There were loud snaps and crackles. The band members stared at the amps with open mouths. Then Spy ran his guitar pick across the strings. No sound came out. Hal did the same with his bass. Silence.

It looked as if Spontaneous Combustion had combusted! And Jessica had a feeling she knew what they were going to say next: *The chick roadie blew it!*

Jessica jumped off the edge of the stage and retreated into the safety of the crowd. *So much for L.A.!* she thought. The battle of the bands had turned into a blowout!

Dana couldn't believe the chaos on the other side of the stage. What had gone wrong with Spontaneous Combustion? She felt sorry for them as she watched the band members deject-edly examining their damaged equipment.

The fans loved the fireworks, though. If anything, they were making more noise over this unexpected show than they had over The Droids' stellar performance. Even the judges were laughing as they put their heads together to confer.

Dana pushed her damp hair off her forehead, giving in to the urge to smile. She didn't wish misfortune on anybody, and she would have preferred to have won the contest fair and square. But she had a feeling that even if Spontaneous Combustion had played their set, and played well, they still wouldn't have had a chance. Tonight, Dana knew, The Droids were unbeatable.

They stood in a row with their arms around each other while they waited for the news: Max, Dana, Guy, Emily, and Dan. Dana was thrilled that they had done so well. But the performance onstage hadn't been half as exciting as the few moments she had spent with Aaron! She couldn't wait to tell Olivia, DeeDee, and Elizabeth about that one. If Elizabeth would still talk to her . . .

The judges had reached a decision. One of them raised a hand to quiet the audience. "The winner of the Sweet Valley battle of the bands," he shouted into a microphone, "by a landslide, is . . . The Droids!"

With exuberant victory shouts, The Droids high-fived and hugged each other. A perfect ending to the happiest night of Dana's life!

Scratch that, Dana thought a moment later when Aaron jumped onto the stage and threw his arms around her. Laughing, she let him twirl her around in a circle. *Now*, this *is a perfect ending!*

Twelve

By the time Monday rolled around, Jessica's spirits had lifted. She had spent almost all day Sunday in bed, recovering from the fatigue of working at the battle of the bands—and the humiliation of being fired by a furious Spy Lazarus, who had managed to track her down after the whole thing was over. He had claimed that she was responsible for the band's failure, and he had called her "one dumb chick."

Jessica didn't care what Spy thought of her, though. She was glad to be rid of the job. "After all, it wasn't the first after-school job I got fired from," she remarked as she and Elizabeth left the Sweet Valley High cafeteria after lunch. "And I hated it—I was going to quit anyway!"

They stopped at Jessica's locker. She twirled the combination idly. "I've figured something out, Liz," she announced.

"What?" Elizabeth asked, getting ready for a laugh. As a rule, there was nothing more entertaining and ridiculous than Jessica's little pearls of wacky wisdom.

"I've been wasting my time," Jessica told her sister. "I mean, my ultimate aim is to meet celebrities and rock stars, right? Well, I'm never going to meet anybody by hanging around with a no-talent high-school band. From now on I'm aiming straight for the top!"

Jessica's locker swung open, and Elizabeth gasped. "What have you done to your locker?"

Jessica viewed her work with a smile of satisfaction. "Nice, isn't it?"

The locker was wallpapered with glossy magazine pictures of her favorite rock star, Jamie Peters. "It looks like some kind of *shrine*," Elizabeth observed.

"Why not?" Jessica said. She gazed at Jamie Peters and sighed. "He *is* an object worthy of worship, if I may say so."

Elizabeth shook her head. "You're nuts, Jess."

"You won't think so someday when my

dream of meeting him comes true," Jessica replied.

"Yeah, but look how disappointed you were in Spy and Spontaneous Combustion," Elizabeth pointed out. "What if Jamie Peters isn't as great as he looks?" Elizabeth leaned closer to inspect the pictures inside the locker. "You know, they airbrush these photos," she teased. "I bet he's actually got wrinkles. That long hair is probably a wig."

Jessica pushed Elizabeth out of the way and slammed the locker shut. "Don't you dare insult Jamie that way!" she warned playfully.

Elizabeth giggled. "Sorry!"

"Just don't do it again," Jessica said. "I have to find Lila now. If she thinks she can get away with ditching me Friday night, she has another think coming!"

"OK—good luck," Elizabeth said. "See you later!"

Elizabeth continued down the corridor, wishing her own mood was as light as Jessica's. She had had a good time at the battle of the bands with Enid and Penny, but there was no pretending. She would have had a much *better* time if Todd had been with her. Instead, Todd had staked out a spot in the bleachers with some of the other basketball players and hadn't once looked in her direction.

The Droids' victory had been thrilling, and Elizabeth had been surprised and delighted when she saw Aaron onstage congratulating Dana with what looked like a more-than-friendly hug. What exactly had it signified? Elizabeth sighed. She would probably never know. Todd wasn't talking to her, and neither was Dana. She'd have to wait to hear the story through the grapevine like everybody else.

Elizabeth opened her locker, and something fell out. She bent to pick it up. It was a white envelope, with her name typed on it. Someone must have stuck it through the slats of the locker and it had fallen down by the inside of the door.

Curious, Elizabeth tore open the envelope. She took out a card depicting a misty, romantic scene. As she opened it, Elizabeth had a funny feeling of déjà vu.

There was a typed message inside. "I love you, Liz, and I'm sorry. Meet me under the clock after school so we can kiss and make up!"

Elizabeth pressed the card to her heart, a joyful smile brightening her face. In an instant, she felt as if the weight of the world had been lifted from her shoulders. She hated being mad at Todd and having him mad at her.

Reading the card again, Elizabeth laughed. Typical Todd. Sending an anonymous love note, when it had been just such a card that got them into trouble in the first place!

The rest of the school day sped by in a blur of anticipation for Elizabeth. Usually she was a model student, but that afternoon the only thing she paid attention to was the clock. When the final bell rang at three, she raced down the hall to the main lobby and pushed eagerly through the front door of the school. Immediately, she saw someone else already standing under the clock. It was Todd!

In a flash, they were in each other's arms. Todd squeezed Elizabeth tightly, lifting her off the ground. Then their lips met in a gentle kiss.

"I'm sorry, Elizabeth," Todd said sincerely.

"No, I'm sorry," she insisted. "I should have seen that you were only trying to help by sending the card to Dana. I was very unfair to you."

"Well, I could have acted a lot more reasonably myself," Todd admitted. He gave Elizabeth a big smile. "But now we're even. You sent your own card, and it's made everything right again!"

Elizabeth tilted her head, confused. "You

mean, you sent *me* a card to make everything right again," she corrected him.

"I didn't send you a card," said Todd, shaking his head. "You sent *me* a card."

"I didn't send you a card!" Elizabeth exclaimed.

They both reached into their pockets to pull out the cards they'd received. Just then, they were distracted by a car honking its horn.

Elizabeth and Todd turned to look at the driveway that ran alongside the school. The car honked again as it drove by slowly. Through the open window, Elizabeth could see two people grinning out at them—Aaron and Dana!

Aaron had one hand on the wheel and his other arm around Dana's shoulders. Anyone could have seen in a glance that they were much more than "just friends."

Todd and Elizabeth waved, smiling.

"I think they just got even with us!" Elizabeth surmised.

"And they returned the favor." Todd tipped Elizabeth's face to his for another kiss. "It looks like we all get a happy ending."

For a long moment, Elizabeth and Todd savored the romance of their reunion. Then Elizabeth pulled back, a mischievous smile on er face. "You know what this means, don't you?"

"What does what mean?" Todd asked.

"Aaron and Dana are a couple! I won the bet!" Elizabeth declared.

"You won the bet," Todd conceded good-naturedly, nodding. "You've earned your three wishes. So what are they going to be?"

"Let's see . . ." Elizabeth thought for a moment. "A dozen roses would be nice, and someone to do my chores and carry my books for a week would be a real treat."

Todd laughed. "I deserve it—I was going to make you wash my car!"

"But after everything that's happened lately, there are *other* things I'd like more." Elizabeth smiled up at him. "Are you ready?"

Todd grinned. "Your wish is my command."

"Then I wish you and I will never have such a pointless argument ever again . . ."

"One," counted Todd.

"And I wish we'll always be together and as happy as we are right now . . ."

"Two." He held up two fingers.

"And I wish you'd give me the biggest, best kiss ever, right this very instant!"

"One Todd Wilkins Deluxe Smooch, coming

right up!" Todd promised as he pulled Eliza beth close.

"Well, Baja Beat didn't win, but you played a fantastic set," Neil Freemount told Andy Jen kins as the two boys cut through the main lobby after school.

"I was happy with our performance," Andy said. "I think we need a little more polish, but we have fun together. I really didn't expect to beat The Droids. I was just glad for a chance to show everyone what we can do. We've already been booked for a party next weekend!"

"Excellent!" remarked Neil.

Out front, the sidewalk was crawling with students heading for the parking lot or climbing aboard buses. Andy and Neil headed for Neil's car. They planned to hit the Dairi Burger on the way home.

Andy was about to tell Neil about the upcom ing gig when someone slammed into his shoul der, knocking him off the curb and into the street.

"Hey, watch where you're walking!" he exclaimed.

"I'll walk where I want," Charlie Cashman said menacingly. "You watch out."

Andy didn't reply. He simply brushed off his shoulder to show his distaste for Charlie. He and Neil continued on their way.

"That guy's a walking bulldozer," Neil observed, shaking his head. "What a jerk!"

"You're telling me," said Andy. "I'm having bad luck with him lately. It seems like everywhere I turn he's there, making some rude comment. I don't know why he hassles me so much."

"I wouldn't worry about it," Neil commented. "I think he acts a lot tougher than he really is."

"I hope so," Andy said, his forehead creased in a puzzled frown. Andy couldn't help feeling the other boy was singling him out for special abuse. What had he ever done to offend Charlie?

Why is Charlie Cashman picking on Andy Jenkins? Find out in SWEET VALLEY HIGH #69, **FRIEND AGAINST FRIEND.**

COULD *YOU* BE THE NEXT SWEET VALLEY READER OF THE MONTH?

ENTER BANTAM BOOKS' SWEET VALLEY CONTEST & SWEEPSTAKES IN ONE!

Calling all Sweet Valley Fans! Here's a chance to appear in a Sweet Valley book!

We know how important Sweet Valley is to you. That's why we've come up with a Sweet Valley celebration offering exciting opportunities to have YOUR thoughts printed in a Sweet Valley book!

"How do I become a Sweet Valley Reader of the Month?"

It's easy. Just write a one-page essay (no more than 150 words, please) telling us a little about yourself, and why you like to read Sweet Valley books. We will pick the best essays and print them along with the winner's photo in the back of upcoming Sweet Valley books. Every month there will be a new Sweet Valley High Reader of the Month!

And, there's more!

Just sending in your essay makes you eligible for the Grand Prize drawing for a trip to Los Angeles, California! This once-in-a-life-time trip includes round-trip airfare, accommodations for 5 nights (economy double occupancy), a rental car, and meal allowances. (Approximate retail value: $4,500.)

Don't wait! Write your essay today.
No purchase necessary. See the next page for Official rules.

ENTER BANTAM BOOKS' SWEET VALLEY READER OF THE MONTH SWEEPSTAKES

OFFICIAL RULES:

READER OF THE MONTH ESSAY CONTEST

1. <u>No Purchase is Necessary.</u> Enter by hand printing your name, address, date of birth and telephone number on a plain 3" x 5" card, and sending this card along with your essay telling us about yourself and why you like to read *Sweet Valley* books to:

READER OF THE MONTH
SWEET VALLEY HIGH
BANTAM BOOKS
YR MARKETING
666 FIFTH AVENUE
NEW YORK, NEW YORK 10103

2. <u>Reader of the Month Contest Winner.</u> For each month from June 1, 1990 through December 31, 1990, a Sweet Valley High Reader of the Month will be chosen from the entries received during that month. The winners will have their essay and photo published in the back of an upcoming Sweet Valley High title.

3. Enter as often as you wish, but each essay must be original and each entry must be mailed in a separate envelope bearing sufficient postage. All completed entries must be postmarked and received by Bantam no later than December 31, 1990, in order to be eligible for the Essay Contest and Sweepstakes. Entrants must be between the ages of 6 and 16 years old. Each essay must be no more than 150 words and must be typed double-spaced or neatly printed on one side of an 8 1/2" x 11" page which has the entrant's name, address, date of birth and telephone number at the top. The essays submitted will be judged each month by Bantam's Marketing Department on the basis of originality, creativity, thoughtfulness, and writing ability, and all of Bantam's decisions are final and binding. Essays become the property of Bantam Books and none will be returned. Bantam reserves the right to edit the winning essays for length and readability. Essay Contest winners will be notified by mail within 30 days of being chosen. In the event there are an insufficient number of essays received in any month which meet the minimum standards established by the judges, Bantam reserves the right not to choose a Reader of the Month. Winners have 30 days from the date of Bantam's notice in which to respond, or an alternate Reader of the Month winner will be chosen. Bantam is not responsible for incomplete or lost or misdirected entries.

4. Winners of the Essay Contest and their parents or legal guardians may be required to execute an Affidavit of Eligibility and Promotional Release supplied by Bantam. Entering the Reader of the Month Contest constitutes permission for use of the winner's name, address, likeness and contest submission for publicity and promotional purposes, with no additional compensation.

5. Employees of Bantam Books, Bantam Doubleday Dell Publishing Group, Inc., and

their subsidiaries and affiliates, and their immediate family members are not eligible to enter the Essay Contest. The Essay Contest is open to residents of the U.S. and Canada (excluding the province of Quebec), and is void wherever prohibited or restricted by law. All applicable federal, state, and local regulations apply.

READER OF THE MONTH SWEEPSTAKES

6. Sweepstakes Entry. No purchase is necessary. Every entrant in the Sweet Valley High, Sweet Valley Twins and Sweet Valley Kids Essay Contest whose completed entry is received by December 31, 1990 will be entered in the Reader of the Month Sweepstakes. The Grand Prize winner will be selected in a random drawing from all completed entries received on or about February 1, 1991 and will be notified by mail. Bantam's decision is final and binding. Odds of winning are dependent on the number of entries received. The prize is non-transferable and no substitution is allowed. The Grand Prize winner must be accompanied on the trip by a parent or legal guardian. Taxes are the sole responsibility of the prize winner. Trip must be taken within one year of notification and is subject to availability. Travel arrangements will be made for the winner and, once made, no changes will be allowed.

7. 1 Grand Prize. A six day, five night trip for two to Los Angeles, California. Includes round-trip coach airfare, accommodations for 5 nights (economy double occupancy), a rental car -- economy model, and spending allowance for meals. (Approximate retail value: $4,500.)

8. The Grand Prize winner and their parent or legal guardian may be required to execute an Affidavit of Eligibility and Promotional Release supplied by Bantam. Entering the Reader of the Month Sweepstakes constitutes permission for use of the winner's name, address, and the likeness for publicity and promotional purposes, with no additional compensation.

9. Employees of Bantam Books, Bantam Doubleday Dell Publishing Group, Inc., and their subsidiaries and affiliates, and their immediate family members are not eligible to enter this Sweepstakes. The Sweepstakes is open to residents of the U.S. and Canada (excluding the province of Quebec), and is void wherever prohibited or restricted by law. If a Canadian resident, the Grand Prize winner will be required to correctly answer an arithmetical skill-testing question in order to receive the prize. All applicable federal, state, and local regulations apply. The Grand Prize will be awarded in the name of the minor's parent or guardian. Taxes, if any, are the winner's sole responsibility.

10. For the name of the Grand Prize winner and the names of the winners of the Sweet Valley High, Sweet Valley Twins and Sweet Valley Kids Essay Contests, send a stamped, self-addressed envelope entirely separate from your entry to: Bantam Books, Sweet Valley Reader of the Month Winners, Young Readers Marketing, 666 Fifth Avenue, New York, New York 10103. The winners list will be available after April 15, 1991.

SWEET VALLEY HIGH

Celebrate the Seasons
with SWEET VALLEY HIGH
Super Editions

You've been a SWEET VALLEY HIGH fan all along—hanging out with Jessica and Elizabeth and their friends at Sweet Valley High. And now the SWEET VALLEY HIGH *Super Editions* give you more of what you like best—more romance—more excitement—more real-life adventure! Whether you're bicycling up the California Coast in PERFECT SUMMER, dancing at the Sweet Valley Christmas Ball in SPECIAL CHRISTMAS, touring the South of France in SPRING BREAK, catching the rays in a MALIBU SUMMER, or skiing the snowy slopes in WINTER CARNIVAL—you know you're exactly where you want to be—with the gang from SWEET VALLEY HIGH.

SWEET VALLEY HIGH SUPER EDITIONS